Elsie's Vacation

The Original Elsie Classics

Elsie Dinsmore
Elsie's Holidays at Roselands
Elsie's Girlhood
Elsie's Womanhood
Elsie's Motherhood
Elsie's Children
Elsie's Widowhood
Grandmother Elsie
Elsie's New Relations
Elsie at Nantucket
The Two Elsies
Elsie's Kith and Kin
Elsie's Friends at Woodburn
Christmas with Grandma Elsie
Elsie and the Raymonds
Elsie Yachting with the Raymonds
Elsie's Vacation
Elsie at Viamede
Elsie at Ion
Elsie at the World's Fair
Elsie's Journey on Inland Waters
Elsie at Home
Elsie on the Hudson
Elsie in the South
Elsie's Young Folks
Elsie's Winter Trip
Elsie and Her Loved Ones
Elsie and Her Namesakes

Elsie's Vacation

Book Seventeen of
The Original Elsie Classics

Martha Finley

CUMBERLAND HOUSE
NASHVILLE, TENNESSEE

Elsie's Vacation
by Martha Finley

Any unique characteristics of this edition:
Copyright © 2000 by Cumberland House Publishing, Inc.

Published by Cumberland House Publishing, Inc.,
431 Harding Industrial Drive, Nashville, Tennessee 37211.

Cover design by Bruce Gore, Gore Studios, Inc.
Photography by Dean Dixon Photography
Hair and Makeup by Calene Rader
Text design by Heather Armstrong

Printed in the United States of America
1 2 3 4 5 6 7 8 — 04 03 02 01 00

CHAPTER FIRST

CAPTAIN RAYMOND went back to the hotel feeling somewhat lonely and heartsore over the parting from his eldest hope, but as he entered the private parlor where his young wife and most of the party were, his look and manner had all their accustomed cheeriness.

He made a pleasant remark to Violet, hugged the little ones, and talked for a few minutes in his usual agreeable way with Mr. and Mrs. Dinsmore and the others; then glancing about the room, as if in search of someone or something, asked, "Where are Lulu and Gracie?"

"Why I thought they were here," Violet answered in some surprise, following the direction of his glance. "They seem to have slipped out of the room so quietly we were unaware."

"I must hunt them up, poor dears! For it is about time we were starting for the *Dolphin*," he said, hastily leaving the room. A low sobbing sound struck upon his ear as he softly opened the door of the room where his little girls had slept the previous night, and there they were down on the carpet near a window, Gracie's head in her sister's lap. Lulu was softly stroking the golden curls and saying in tender tones, "Don't, Gracie, dear; oh, don't! It can't be helped, you know. We have our dear papa and Mamma Vi, and the little ones left. Besides, Maxie will come home again to visit us very soon."

"Oh, but he'll never live at home with us any more," sobbed Gracie. "At least I'm afraid he won't, and—and, oh, I do love him so! And he's the only big brother we have."

"But we have papa, dear, dear papa, who used to be obliged to go away and leave us, but we have him all the time now," Lulu replied half chokingly. "I wish we could have them both, but we can't, and we both do love papa the best after all."

"And papa loves his two dear little girls more than tongue can tell," the captain said in tenderest tones, drawing near and bending down to take both in his arms together. He kissed first one and then the other. "Be comforted, my darlings," he went on, holding them close to his heart. "We haven't lost our Maxie by any means, and though I left him feeling a trifle homesick and forlorn, he will get over that in a day or two, I know, and greatly enjoy the business of preparing himself for the life work he has freely chosen."

"But, oh, papa, how he will miss our lovely home, and you, and all of us!" sobbed Gracie, hiding her tear-stained face on her father's shoulder.

"Not as you would, my darling," he replied, holding her close and caressing her with great tenderness. "Boys are different from girls, and I think our dear Maxie will soon feel very happy there among his mates, though he will, I am sure, never cease to love his father, sisters, Mamma Vi, baby brother, and his home with them all."

"Papa, I'm thinking how he'll miss the pleasant evenings at home and the good talks with you," sobbed the little girl.

"Yes, darling, but I will tell you what we will do to partly, at least, make up for that loss to our dear boy."

"What, papa?" she asked, lifting her head and looking up into his face with her own brightening a little.

"Suppose we each keep a journal or diary, telling everything that goes on each day at home, and now and then we can send them to Maxie, so that he will know all that we are doing?"

"Oh, what a good thought, papa!" exclaimed Lulu, giving him a vigorous hug and kiss. "And Maxie will write us nice, interesting letters. One of these days he'll come home for a visit and have ever so much to tell us."

"Yes," her father said. "And I think we will have interesting letters from him in the meantime."

"And perhaps I'll learn to like writing letters, when it's just to please Maxie and comfort him," said Gracie, wiping away her tears and trying her very best to smile.

"I hope so, darling," her father replied, bestowing another kiss upon the sweet, little tear-stained face. "But now, my dears," he added, "put on your hats. It is time to go back to the *Dolphin*."

They hastened to obey, and he led them to the parlor, where they found the rest of the party ready to accompany them on board the yacht.

The sun was setting as they reached the *Dolphin's* deck, and they found a luxurious repast ready for them to partake of by the time outdoor garments could be laid aside and wind-tossed hair restored to order.

The captain missed the bright face of his firstborn at the table, but, exerting himself for the entertainment of the others, seemed even more than usually cheery and genial, now and then indulging in some innocent jest that made his little girls laugh in spite of themselves. At length they almost forgot, for the moment, their parting from Max, their grief over the thought that he would no longer share their lessons or their sports and would only be at home after what, in the prospect, seemed to them a long, long time—and then but for a little while.

On leaving the table all gathered upon deck. There was no wind, but the yacht had a steam engine and used her sails only on occasions when they could be of service. Stars shone brightly in the sky overhead, but their light was not sufficient to give an extended view on land or water. As all were weary with the excitement and sightseeing of the day, they retired early to their berths.

Poor Gracie, worn out with this rather unusual excitement, and especially the grief of the parting with Max, was asleep the instant her head touched the pillow. Not so with Lulu. Her loneliness and depression banished sleep from her eyes for the time, and presently she slipped from her berth, threw on a warm dressing gown, and thrust her feet into felt slippers. The next moment she stole noiselessly into the salon where her father sat alone looking over an evening paper.

He was not aware of her entrance till she stood close at his side, her hand on his shoulder, her eyes fixed with a gaze of ardent affection upon his face.

"Dear child!" he said, looking up from his paper and smiling affectionately upon her. He tossed the paper aside, put an arm about her waist, drew her to his knee, and pressed fatherly kisses upon lip and cheek and brow, asking tenderly if anything was wrong with her that she had come in search of him when he supposed her to be already in bed and sound asleep.

"I'm not sick, papa," she said in reply. "But, oh, I miss Maxie so!" The words were almost a sob, and she clung about her father's neck, hiding her face on his shoulder.

"I, too, miss my boy more than words can tell," he replied, stroking her hair with a gently caressing touch, and she was sure his tones trembled a little with the pain of the thought of Max, left alone among strangers. "But I thank God, our heavenly Father, that I have by no means lost my eldest son, while I still have another one and three dear daughters to add to my happiness in our sweet home.'

"I do want to add to it, you dear, dear, good papa!" she said, hugging and kissing him over and over again. "Oh, I wish I was a better girl for your sake, so that my wrong-doing would never give you pain!"

"I think—and am very happy in the thought—that you are improving," he said, repeating his caresses. "It is a great comfort to me," he continued, "that my little girls need not be sent away from home and their father to be educated."

"To me also, papa," she returned. "I am very thankful that I may live with my dear father always while we are spared to each other. I don't mean to ever go away from you, papa, but to stay with you always, to wait on you and do everything I can do to be a great help, comfort, and blessing to you—even when I'm grown up to womanhood."

"Ah!" he returned, again smoothing her hair caressingly and smiling down into her eyes, but then holding her close. "I shall be very glad to keep you as long as you may prefer life with me, my own dear, dear child," he said in tender tones. "I look upon my dear, eldest daughter as one of the great blessings my Heavenly Father has bestowed upon me, and which I hope He may spare to me as long as I live."

"Papa, I'm so, so glad you love me so dearly!" she exclaimed, lifting to his eyes full of love and joy. "And, oh, I do love you so! I want to be a great blessing to you as long as we both live."

"I don't doubt it, my darling," he replied. "I doubt neither your desire nor purpose to be such."

"Yes, sir, I do really long to be the very greatest of comforts to you, and yet," she sighed, "I have such a bad temper you know, papa, I'm so willful, too, that—that I'm afraid—almost sure, indeed—I'll be naughty again one of these days and give you the pain of punishing me for it."

"That would grieve me very much, but would not diminish my love for you," he said, "nor yours for me, I think."

"No, indeed, papa!" she exclaimed, creeping closer into his embrace. "Because I know that when you have to punish me in any way it makes you very, very sorry."

"It does indeed!" he responded.

"Papa," she sighed, "I'm always dreadfully sorry and ashamed after one of my times of being disobedient, willful, and ill-tempered, and I am really thankful to you for taking so much pains and trouble to make a better girl of me."

"I don't doubt it, daughter," he answered. "It is a long while now since I have had any occasion to punish you, and your conduct has rarely called for even so much as a reproof."

She gave him a glad, grateful look, an embrace of ardent affection, then, laying her cheek to his, "You dear, dear papa, you have made me feel very happy," she said. "I'm sure I am much happier that I should be if you had let me go on indulging my bad temper and willfulness. Oh, it's so nice to be able to run to my dear father whenever I want to, and always to be so kindly received that I can't feel any doubt that he loves me dearly. Ah, how I pity poor Maxie that he can't see you for weeks or months!"

"And don't you pity papa a little that he can't see Maxie?" he asked with a smile and a sigh.

"Oh, yes! Yes, indeed! I'm so sorry for you, papa, and I mean to do all I can to supply his place. What do you suppose Maxie is doing just now, papa?"

"Doubtless he is in his room preparing his lessons for tomorrow. The bugle call for evening study hour sounds at half-past seven, and the lads must be busy with their books till half-past nine."

He drew out his watch, and glancing at its face, said, "Ah, it is just nine o'clock," he said. "Kiss me goodnight, daughter, and go back to your berth."

CHAPTER SECOND

Max was in his room at the Academy, busy with his tasks, trying determinately to forget homesickness by giving his whole mind to them and succeeding fairly well. Very desirous, very determined was the lad to acquit himself to the very best of his ability that he might please and honor both his Heavenly Father and his earthly one.

By the time the welcome sound of gunfire and tattoo announced that the day's work was over he felt fully prepared for the morrow's recitations, but he was in no mood for play. The quiet that had reigned through the building for the last two hours was suddenly broken in upon by sounds of mirth and jollity—merry boyish voices talking, singing, some accompanying themselves with the twang of a banjo or the tinkle of a guitar. But Max, closing and putting his book aside, kept his seat, his elbow on the desk, his head on his hand, while with a far-away look in his dark eyes, he indulged in a waking dream.

He seemed to see the *Dolphin* steaming down the bay, his father perhaps, sitting in the salon with the other grown folks—he was pretty sure the younger ones would have retired to their state-rooms—and thinking and speaking of his absent son. Or, it might be, pacing the deck alone, his heart going up in prayer to God for his firstborn, his "might and the beginning of his strength," that he might be kept from sin and every danger and evil and enabled to prove himself a brave, true follower of Christ, never ashamed or afraid to show his colors and let it be known to all with whom he had to do that he was a disciple — a servant of the dear Lord Jesus.

"Lord, help me. Help me to be brave and faithful and true," was the silent petition that went up from the boy's heart.

"Homesick, bub?" asked a boyish voice in somewhat mocking tones. "I believe most of the fellows are just at the first, but they get over it after a bit without much doctoring."

"I'm inclined to think it is not a dangerous kind of ailment," returned Max in a pleasant tone, lifting his head and turning toward his companion with a smile that seemed rather forced. "However, I was thinking not of home, exactly, but the homefolks who are just at present aboard my father's yacht and steaming down the bay."

It was only by a great effort he repressed a sigh with the concluding words.

"That's a handsome yacht and about the largest I ever saw," was the next remark of his roommate — Benjamin Hunt by name — of about the same age as himself, not particularly handsome but with a good, honest face.

"Yes, and she's a splendid sailer," returned Max. "Papa bought her this summer, and we've had a good time sailing or steaming — sometimes one and again the other, the *Dolphin* has both sails and engines — along the coast and a short distance out to sea."

"Did she have a good captain?" Hunt asked with a quizzical smile.

"My father, a retired naval officer. There could be none better," returned Max, straightening himself slightly, while the color deepened on is cheek.

"Yes, I don't wonder you are proud of him," laughed Hunt. "I happened to see him when he brought you here, and I must say I thought he had a fine military bearing and was — well, I think I might say — one of the handsomest men I ever saw."

"Thank you," said Max heartily, glancing up at Hunt with a gratified smile. "I suppose being so fond of him I may not be a competent judge, but to me my father seems the best, the noblest, and the handsomest man that ever lived."

"Didn't force you to come here against your will, eh?" queried Hunt jestingly.

"No, indeed! He only let me come because I wanted to. I think he would have been glad if I had chosen the ministry. But you see I don't think I have any talent in that line, and I inherit a love for the sea. Papa says a man can do best in the profession or business that is most to his taste, so that perhaps I may be more useful as a naval officer than I could be in the ministry."

"Especially in case of war, and if you turn out a good and capable commander," returned Hunt, tossing a ball and catching it as it fell. "I sometimes think I'd like nothing better. A fellow would have a chance to distinguish himself, such as he could never hope for in time of peace."

"Yes; and if such a thing should happen I hope it will be when I'm ready to take part in the defense of my country," said Max, his cheek flushing and his eyes kindling. "But war is an awful thing considering all the killing and maiming, to say nothing of the destruction of property, and I hope our country will never be engaged in another. But, excuse me," he added, opening his Bible, "I see we have scarcely fifteen minutes now before taps will sound."

At that Hunt moved away to his own side of the room from whence he watched Max furtively, a mocking smile on his lips.

Max was uncomfortably conscious of it, but he tried to ignore it and give his thoughts to what he was reading. Presently, closing his book, he knelt and silently offered up his evening prayer, asking forgiveness of all his sins, strength to resist temptation, and never be afraid or ashamed to own himself a follower of Jesus, His loving disciple, his servant, whose greatest desire was to know and do the Master's will. Very earnestly he prayed that no evil might befall his dearly loved and honored father, his sisters or brother, Mamma Vi, or any of those he loved; that they might be taken safely through all their journeying, and he permitted to see them all again when the right time should come; and having committed both them and himself to the watchful care of his Heavenly Father, he rose from his knees and began his preparations for bed.

"Well, soon, I hope you will sleep soundly and well after saying your prayers like the goodest of little boys," sneered Hunt.

"I shall sleep none the worse," returned Max pleasantly despite the sneer.

"I'll bet not a bit better than I shall without going through any such babylike performance."

"God is very good and often takes care of those who don't ask Him to," said Max. "But I don't think they have any right to expect it. Also I am sure I should be shamefully ungrateful if I were to lie down for my night's rest without a word of thanks to Him for His protecting care over me and mine through the day that is just past. As to its being a babylike performance, it is one in which some of the greatest, as well as best men, have indulged. Washington was a man of prayer. So was General Daniel Morgan—that grand revolutionary officer who whipped Tarleton so completely at the battle of the Cowpens. There was Macdonough also, who gained that splendid victory over the British on Lake Champlain in the war of 1812–14. Have you forgotten that just before the fight began, after he had put springs on his cables, had the decks cleared, and everything was ready for action with his officers and men around him, he knelt down near one of his heaviest guns and in a few words asked God to help him in the coming struggle? He might well do that, because, as you know of course, we were in the right, fighting against oppression and wrongs fit to rouse the indignation of the most patient and forbearing of mortals."

"That's a fact!" interrupted Hunt. "Americans have always been forbearing at the start, but let them get once thoroughly roused and they made things hot enough for the aggressors."

"So they do," said Max. "And so I think they always will. I hope so, anyhow, for I don't believe it's right for any nation to allow any of its people to be so dreadfully wronged and ill-treated as thousands of our poor sailors were, by the English, before the war of 1812 taught them better. I don't believe the mass of the English people approved, but they couldn't keep their aristocracy—who hated republicanism and wanted always to continue superior in station and power to the mass of their countrymen and ours—from oppressing and abusing our poor sailors, impressing, flogging, and ill-treating them in various ways, and to such a degree that it makes one's blood boil in reading or thinking of it. And I think it's right enough for one to be angry and indignant at such wrongs to others."

"Of course it is," said Hunt. "Americans always will resist oppression—of themselves or their weaker brethren—and I glory in the fact. What a fight that was of Macdonough's! Do you remember the incident of the gamecock?"

"No. What was it?"

"It seems that one of the shots from the British vessel *Linnet* demolished a hencoop on the deck of the *Saratoga*, releasing this gamecock, and that he flew to a gunslide, where he alighted, then clapped his wings and crowed lustily.

"That delighted our sailors, who accepted the incident as an omen of the victory that crowned their arms before the fight was over. They cheered and felt their courage strengthened."

"Good!" said Max. "That chicken was at better business than the fighting he had doubtless been brought up to."

> "'O Johnny Bull, my joe John,
> Behold on Lake Champlain,
> With more than equal force, John,
> You tried your fist again;
> But the cock saw how 'twas going,
> And cried 'Cock-a-doodle-doo,'
> And Macdonough was victorious,
> Johnny Bull, my joe!'"

"Pretty good," laughed Max. "But there are the taps; so goodnight."

CHAPTER THIRD

LULU WOKE EARLY the next morning and was dressed and on deck before any other of the *Dolphin's* passengers. Day had dawned and the eastern sky was bright with purple, orange, and gold, heralding the near approach of the sun which, just as she set foot on the deck, suddenly showed his face above the restless waves, making a golden pathway across them.

"Oh, how very beautiful!" came her involuntary exclamation. Then catching sight of her father standing with his back toward her, and apparently absorbed in gazing upon the sunrise, she hastened to his side, caught his hand in hers, and carried it to her lips with a glad, "Good morning, you dear papa."

"Ah! Good morning, my darling," he returned, bending down to press a kiss on the bright, upturned face.

"Such a lovely morning, papa, isn't it?" she said, standing with her hand fast clasped in his and turning her eyes again upon sea and sky. "But where are we now? Almost at Fort Monroe?"

"Look and tell me what you see," was his smiling rejoinder, as, with a hand on each of her shoulders, he turned her about so she caught the view from the other side of the vessel.

"Oh, papa, is that it?" she exclaimed. "Why, we're almost there, aren't we?"

"Yes, we will reach our anchorage within a few minutes, Lulu."

"Oh, are we going to stop to see the old fort, papa?" she asked eagerly.

"I think we are," was his smiling rejoinder. "But you don't expect to find in it a relic of the Revolution, do you?" he asked laughingly, pinching her cheek, then bending down to kiss again the rosy face upturned to his.

"Why, yes, papa. I have been thinking there must have been a fight there. Wasn't that the case?"

"No, daughter. The fortress was not there at that time."

"Was it in the war of 1812, then, papa?"

"No," he returned, smiling down on her. "The building of Fortress Monroe was not begun until 1817. However, there was a small fort built on Point Comfort in 1630, and also, shortly before the siege of Yorktown, Count de Grasse had some fortifications thrown up to protect his troops in landing to take part in that affair."

Just then their talk was interrupted by the coming on deck of one after another of their party and the exchange of morning greetings; then followed the interest and excitement of the approach to the fortress and anchoring in its vicinity.

Next came the call to breakfast. But naturally, and quite to Lulu's satisfaction, the talk at the table turned upon the building of the fort, its history and that of the adjacent country, particularly Hampton, two and a half miles distant.

The captain pointed it out to them all as they stood upon the deck shortly afterward.

"Papa, can you please tell me which is Old Point Comfort?" asked Gracie.

"That sandy promontory on the extremity of which stands Fortress Monroe," he answered. "Yonder, on the opposite side, is Point Willoughby, the two forming the mouth of the James River, and these are the Rip Raps between the two. You see that there the ocean tides and the currents of the river meet and cause a constant ripple. There is a narrow channel of deep water through the bar, but elsewhere between the capes it is shallow.

"Beyond the Rip Raps we see the spacious harbor which is called Hampton Roads. It is so large that great navies might ride there together."

"And I think some have ridden there in our wars with England?" remarked Rosie, half inquiringly.

"You are quite right," replied the captain. "That happened in both the Revolution and the last war with England.

"In October, 1775, Lord Dunmore, the British governor of Virginia who had, however, abdicated some months earlier by fleeing on board a man-of-war, the *Fowey*, driven by his fears and his desire for revenge to destroy the property of the patriots, sent Captain Squires of the British navy with six tenders into Hampton Creek.

"He reached there before the arrival of Colonel Woodford, who with a hundred Culpeper men, had been sent to protect the people of Hampton. Captain Squires sent armed men in boats to burn the town, protecting them by a furious cannonade from the guns of the tenders.

"But they were baffled in the carrying out of their design, being driven off by Virginia riflemen concealed in their houses. Excellent marksmen those Virginians were, and they picked off so many of the advancing foe that they felt compelled to take ignominious flight to their boats and return to the vessels, which then had to withdraw beyond the reach of the rifles to await reinforcements."

"What is a tender, papa?" asked Gracie, as her father paused in his narrative.

"A small vessel that attends on a larger one to convey intelligence and supply stores," he replied and then went on with his account of Dunmore's great repulse.

"Woodford and his men reached Hampton about daybreak of the succeeding morning. At sunrise they saw the hostile fleet approaching. It came so near as to be within rifle shot, and Woodford bade his men fire with caution, taking sure aim. They obeyed and picked off so many from every part of the vessels that the seamen were soon seized with a great terror. The cannons were silenced—the men who worked them being shot down—and their commander presently ordered a retreat. But that was difficult to accomplish, for anyone seen at the helm, or aloft, adjusting the sails, was sure to become a target for the sharpshooters. In consequence many of the sailors retreated to the holds of the vessels, and when their commander ordered them out on the dangerous duty, refused to obey.

"The victory for the Americans was complete; before the fleet could escape, the Hampton people, with Woodford and his soldiers, had sunk five vessels."

"Such a victory!" exclaimed Rosie.

"Yes," the captain said, smiling at her enthusiasm.

"Were the houses they fired on the very ones that are there now, papa?" asked Lulu.

"Some few of them," he replied. "Nearly all were burned by Magruder in the Civil War, among them St. John's Episcopal Church, which was built probably about 1700. Before the Revolution it bore the royal arms carved upon its steeple, but soon after the Declaration of Independence—so it is said—that steeple was struck by lightning and those badges of royalty were hurled to the ground."

"Just as the country was shaking off the yoke they represented," laughed Rosie. "A good omen, wasn't it, Brother Levis?"

"So it would seem, viewed in the light of after events," he answered with a smile.

"Papa, can't we visit Hampton?" asked Lulu rather eagerly.

"Yes, if you would all like to do so," was the reply in an indulgent tone and with an inquiring glance at the older members of the party.

Everyone seemed to think it would be a pleasant little excursion, especially as the *Dolphin* would carry them all the way to the town. But first they must visit the fortress. They did not, however, set out thither immediately, but all remained on the deck a little longer gazing about and questioning the captain in regard to the points of interest.

"Papa," asked Gracie, pointing in a southerly direction, "is that another fort yonder?"

"Yes," he replied. "That is Fort Wool. It is a mile distant. With Fortress Monroe, it defends Hampton Roads, the Gosport navy yard, and Norfolk."

"They both have soldiers in them?" she asked.

"Yes, daughter. Both contain barracks for the soldiers, and Fortress Monroe has also an arsenal, a United States school of artillery, chapel, and, besides the barracks for the soldiers, storehouses and other buildings. It covers over eighty acres of ground."

"And when was it finished, papa? How long did it take to build it?"

"It is not finished yet," he answered. "It has already cost nearly three million dollars. It is an irregular hexagon—that is, has six sides and six angles—surrounded by a tide-water ditch eight feet deep at high water."

"I see trees and some flower gardens, papa," she remarked.

"Yes," he said. "There are a good many trees, standing singly and in groves. The flower gardens belong to the officers' quarters. Now, if you will make yourselves ready for the trip, ladies, Mr. Dinsmore, and any of you younger ones who care to go," he added, smoothing Gracie's golden curls with a caressing hand and smiling down into her face, "we will take a nearer view."

No one felt disposed to decline the invitation, and they were soon on their way to the fortress.

It did not take very long to look at all they cared to see, then they returned to the vessel, weighed anchor, and passed through the narrow channel of the Rip Raps into the spacious harbor of Hampton Roads.

It was a lovely day and all were on deck, enjoying the breeze and the prospect on both land and water.

"Papa," said Lulu, "you haven't told us yet what happened here in the last war with England."

"No," he said. "They attacked Hampton by both land and water, a force of twenty-five hundred men under General Beckwith, landing at Old Point Comfort and marching from there against the town, while at the same time Admiral Cockburn assailed it from the water.

"The fortification at Hampton was but slight and was guarded by only four hundred and fifty militiamen. Feeling themselves too weak to repel an attack by such overwhelming odds, they retired, and the town was given up to pillage."

"Didn't they do any fighting at all, papa?" asked Lulu in a tone of regret and mortification. "I know Americans often did fight when their numbers were very much smaller than those of the enemy."

"That is quite true," he said with a gleam of patriotic pride in his eye. "And sometimes won the victory in spite of the odds against them. That thing had happened only a few days previously at Craney Island, and the British were doubtless smarting under a sense of humiliating defeat when they proceeded to the attack of Hampton."

"How many of the British were there, captain?" asked Evelyn Leland. "I have forgotten, though I know they far outnumbered the Americans."

"Yes," he replied. "As I have said, there were about four hundred fifty Americans, while Beckwith had twenty-five hundred men and was assisted by the flotilla of Admiral Cockburn, consisting of armed boats and barges, which appeared suddenly off Blackbeard's Point at the mouth of Hampton creek at the same time that Beckwith's troops moved stealthily forward through the woods under the cover of the *Mohawk's* guns.

"To draw the attention of the Americans from the land force coming against them was Cockburn's object, in which he was partly successful, his flotilla being seen first by the American patrols at Mill Creek.

"They gave the alarm, arousing the camp, and a line of battle was formed. But just then someone came in haste to tell them of the large land force coming against the town from the rear. Presently in the woods and grain fields could be seen the scarlet uniforms of the British and the green ones of the French."

"Oh, how frightened the people in the town must have been!" exclaimed Gracie. "I should think they'd all have run away."

"Most of them did," replied her father. "But some sick and feeble ones had to stay behind—others also in whose care they were—and trust to the supposed humanity of the British, which proved to be a vain reliance, at least so far as Admiral Cockburn was concerned. He gave up the town to pillage and rapine, allowing the doing of such deeds as have consigned his name to well-merited infamy.

"But to return to my story: Major Crutchfield, the American commander, resolved that he and his four hundred fifty men would do what they could to defend the town. They were encamped on an estate called Little England, a short distance southwest of Hampton, and had a heavy battery of seven guns, the largest an eighteen-pound cannon.

"Major Crutchfield was convinced that the intention of the British was to make their principal attack in his rear, and that Cockburn's was only a feint to draw his attention from the other. So he sent Captain Servant out with his rifle company to ambush on the road by which Beckwith's troops were approaching, ordering him to attack and check the enemy. Then when Cockburn came round Blackbeard's Point and opened fire on the American camp, he received so warm a welcome from Crutchfield's heavy battery that he was presently glad to escape for shelter behind the Point and content himself with throwing an occasional shot or rocket into the American camp.

"Beckwith's troops had reached rising ground and halted for breakfast before the Americans discovered them. When that happened Sergeant Parker, with a fieldpiece and a few picked men, went to the assistance of Captain Servant and his rifle company, already lying in ambush.

"Parker had barely time to reach his position and plant his cannon when the British were seen rapidly advancing.

"At the head of the west branch of Hampton creek, at Celey Road, there was a large cedar tree behind which Servant's advanced corps — Lieutenant Hope and two other men — had stationed themselves. Just as the British crossed the creek — the French column in the front, led by the British sergeant major — they opened a deadly fire upon them. A number were killed, among them the sergeant major — a large, powerful man.

"This threw the British ranks into great confusion for a time, and the main body of our riflemen delivered their fire, killing the brave Lieutenant-Colonel Williams of the British army. But the others presently recovered from their panic and pushed forward, while our riflemen, being so few in number, were compelled to fall back.

"But Crutchfield had heard the firing, and he hastened forward with nearly all his force, leaving Pryor and his artillerymen behind to defend the Little England estate from the attack of the barges. But while he was moving along the lane that led to the plantation toward Celey Road and the great highway, he was suddenly assailed by an enfilading fire from the left.

"Instantly he ordered his men to wheel and charge upon the foe, who were now in the edge of the woods. His troops obeyed, behaving like veterans, and the enemy fell back. Presently they rallied, and showing themselves directly in front of the Americans, opened upon them in a storm of grape and canister from two six-pounders and some Congreve rockets.

"The Americans stood the storm for a few minutes, then fell back, broke ranks, and some of them fled in confusion.

"In the meantime Parker had been working his piece with good effect till his ammunition gave out. Lieutenant Jones of the Hampton artillery, perceiving that to be the case, hurried to his assistance, but seeing an overwhelming force of the enemy approaching, they—Parker's men—fell back to the Yorktown Pike.

"Jones, who had one cannon with him, found that his match had gone out. Rushing to a house near by, he snatched a burning brand from the fire, hurried back, and hid himself in a hollow near a spring.

"The British supposed they had captured all the cannon, or that if any were left they had been abandoned. Drawing near they presently filled the lane; then Jones rose and discharged his piece with terrible effect, many of the British were prostrated by the unexpected shot. During the confusion that followed, Jones made good his retreat, attaching a horse to his cannon and bearing it off with him.

"He hastened to the assistance of Pryor, but on drawing near his camp saw that it had fallen into the possession of the foe.

"Pryor had retreated to safety after spiking his guns. He and his command fought their way through the enemy's ranks with their guns and swam the west branch of Hampton Creek. Making a circuit in the enemy's rear, they fled without losing a man or a musket.

"Jones had seen it all, and spiking his gun, he followed Pryor's men to the same place.

"In the meantime Crutchfield had rallied his men, those who still remained with him, on the flank of Servant's riflemen and was again fighting rather vigorously.

"But presently a powerful flank movement of the foe showed him that he was in danger of being cut off from his line of retreat. He then withdrew in good order and escaped, though pursued for two miles by the enemy.

"That ended the battle, in which about thirty Americans and fifty British had fallen. Then presently followed the disgraceful scenes in Hampton of which I have already told you as having brought lasting infamy upon the name of Sir George Cockburn."

"I think he was worse than a savage!" exclaimed Lulu hotly.

"Certainly, far worse. And more brutal than some of the Indian chiefs—Brand, for instance," said Rosie, "or Tecumseh."

"I cannot see in what respect he was any better than a pirate," added Evelyn in a quiet tone.

"Nor can I," said Captain Raymond. "So very shameful were his atrocities that even the most violent of his British partisans were constrained to denounce them."

CHAPTER FOURTH

BEFORE THE SUN had set the *Dolphin* was again speeding over the water, but now on the ocean, and going northward, Philadelphia being their present destination. It had grown cloudy and by bedtime a steady rain was falling, but unaccompanied by much wind, so that no one felt any apprehension of shipwreck or other marine disaster, and all slept well.

The next morning Lulu was, as usual, one of the first to leave her berth, and having herself neat for the day, she hurried upon deck.

It had ceased raining, and the clouds were breaking away.

"Oh, I'm so glad!" she exclaimed, running to meet her father, who was coming toward her, holding out his hand with an affectionate smile. "I'm so glad it is clearing off so beautifully. Aren't you, papa?"

"Yes, particularly for your sake, daughter," he replied, putting an arm about her and bending down to give her a good morning kiss. "Did you sleep well?"

"Yes, indeed, papa, thank you. But I woke early and got up because I wanted to come on deck and look about. Where are we now? I can see land on the western side."

"Yes, that is a part of the Delaware coast," he answered. "We are nearing Cape Henlopen. Do you remember what occurred near there, at the village of Lewes, in the war of 1812?"

"No, sir," she said. "Won't you please tell me about it?"

"I will. It's not a very long story. It was in March of the year 1813 that the British, after destroying such small merchant craft as they could find in Chesapeake Bay, concluded to blockade Delaware Bay and River and reduce to submission the Americans living along their shores. Commodore Beresford was accordingly sent on the expedition in command of the *Belvidera, Poictiers,* and several smaller vessels.

"On the sixteenth of March he appeared before Lewes in his vessel, the *Poictiers,* and pointing her guns toward the town, sent a note addressed to the first magistrate demanding twenty live bullocks and a proportionate quantity of hay and vegetables for the use of his Britannic majesty's squadron. He offered to pay for them, but he threatened in the event of refusal to destroy the town."

"The insolent fellow!" cried Lulu. "I hope they didn't do it, papa?"

"No, indeed, they flatly refused compliance and told him to do his worst. The people on both sides of the bay and river had heard of his approach and armed bodies of them were gathered at points where an attack might be expected. There were still among them some of the old soldiers of the Revolution, and you may be sure they were ready to do their best to repel the second invasion by their old enemy. One of these was a bent old man of the name of Jonathan M'Nult. He lived in Dover, and when, on the Sabbath day, the drums beat to arms, he, along with men of every denomination to the number of nearly five hundred, quickly responded to the call, took part in the drill, and spent the whole afternoon in making ball cartridges.

"The people of all the towns of the vicinity showed the same spirit and turned out with spades and muskets, ready to take part in the throwing up of batteries and trenches or to fight 'for their altars and their fires' — defending wives, children, and other helpless ones. At Wilmington they built a strong fort which they named Union.

"This spirited and sudden behavior of the Americans surprised Beresford, and for three weeks he refrained from any attempt to carry out his threat.

"During that time Governor Haslet came to Lewes and summoned the militia to its defense. On his arrival he reiterated the refusal to supply the British invaders with what had been demanded.

"Beresford repeated his threats and at length, on the sixth of April, sent Captain Byron with the *Belvidera* and several smaller vessels to attack the town.

"He fired several heavy round shot into it, then sent a flag of truce, again demanding the supplies Beresford had called for.

"Colonel Davis, the officer in command of the militia, repeated the refusal. Then Byron sent word that he was sorry for the misery he should inflict on the women and children by a bombardment.

"To that a verbal reply was sent: 'Colonel Davis is a gallant officer and has taken care of the ladies.'

"Then Byron presently began a cannonade and bombardment and kept it up for twenty-two hours.

"The Americans replied in a spirited manner from a battery on an eminence. Davis's militia worked it and succeeded in disabling the most dangerous of the enemy's gunboats and silencing its cannon.

"The British failed in their effort to inflict great damage upon the town, although they hurled into it as many as eight hundred eighteen- and thirty-two-pound shot, besides many shells and Congreve rockets. The heavy round shot injured some of the homes but the shells did not reach the town. The rockets passed over it. No one was killed.

"Plenty of powder was sent for the American guns from DuPont's at Wilmington, and they picked up and sent back the British balls, which they found just fitted their cannon."

"How good that was," laughed Lulu. "It reminds me of the British at Boston asking the Americans to sell them their balls which they had picked up, and the Americans answering, 'Give us powder and we'll return your balls.' But is that all of your story, papa?"

"Yes, all about the fight at Lewes, but on the afternoon of the next day the British tried to land to steal some of the livestock in the neighborhood, yet without success, as the American militia met them at the water's edge and drove them back to their ships.

"About a month later the British squadron dropped down to Newbold's Pond, seven miles below Lewes, and boats filled with their armed men were sent ashore for water, but a few of Colonel Davis's men, met and drove them back to their ships. So, finding he could not obtain supplies on the Delaware shore, Beresford's little squadron sailed for Bermuda."

"Good! Thank you for telling me about it, papa," said Lulu. "Are we going to stop at Lewes?"

"No, but we will pass near enough to have a distant view of the town."

"Oh, I want to see it!" she exclaimed. "I'm sure the rest will when they hear what happened there."

"Well, daughter, there will be nothing to hinder," the captain answered pleasantly.

"How soon will we reach the point from which we can see it best, papa?" she asked.

"I think about the time we leave the breakfast table," was his reply.

"Papa, don't you miss Max?"

"Very much," he said. "Dear boy! He is doubtless feeling quite lonely and homesick this morning. However, he will soon get over that and enjoy his studies and his sports."

"I think he'll do you credit, papa, and make us proud of him," she said, slipping her hand into her father's and looking lovingly into his face.

"Yes," the captain said, pressing the little hand affectionately in his. "I have no doubt he will. I think, as I am sure his sister Lulu does, that Max is a boy any father and sister might be proud of."

"Yes, indeed, papa!" she responded. "I'm glad he is my brother, and I hope to live to see him an admiral, as I'm sure you would have been if you had stayed in the navy and we'd had a war."

"And if my partial little daughter had the bestowal of such preferment and titles," he added laughingly.

Rosie and Evelyn had joined them, followed almost immediately by Walter and Gracie, when Lulu gave them in a few hasty sentences the information her father had given her in regard to the history of Lewes and told of their near approach to it.

Everyone was interested and all hurried from the breakfast table to the deck in time to catch a view of the place, though a rather distant one.

When it had vanished from sight, Evelyn turned to Captain Raymond, exclaiming, "Oh, sir, will you not point out Forts Mercer and Mifflin to us when we come in sight of them?"

"With pleasure," he replied. "They are at Red Bank. Fort Mercer on the New Jersey shore of the Delaware River, a few miles below Philadelphia, Fort Mifflin on the other side of the river on Great and Little Mud Islands. It was, in Revolutionary days, a strong redoubt with quite extensive outworks."

"Did our men fight the British there in the Revolutionary War, papa?" asked Gracie.

"Yes. It was in the fall of 1777, soon after the battle of the Brandywine in which, as you may remember, the Americans were defeated. They retreated to Chester that night, marched the next day toward Philadelphia, and encamped near Germantown. Howe followed and took possession of the city of Philadelphia.

"The Americans, fearing such an event, had put obstructions in the Delaware River to prevent the British ships from ascending it, and they also had built these two forts with which to protect the *chevaux-de-frise*.

"The battle of the Brandywine, you may remember, was fought on the eleventh of September, and, as I have said, the British pushed on to Philadelphia and entered it in triumph on the twenty-sixth."

"Papa, what are *chevaux-de-frise*?" asked Gracie.

"They are ranges of strong frames with iron pointed wooden spikes," he answered, then went on with his story.

"In addition to these, the Americans had erected batteries on the shores, among which was the strong redoubt called Fort Mercer, which, along with Fort Mifflin on the Mud islands, I have already mentioned. Besides all these, there were several floating batteries and armed galleys stationed in the river.

"All this troubled the British general, because he foresaw that their presence there would make it very difficult, if not impossible, to keep his army supplied with provisions. They would also be in more danger from the American forces if unsupported by their fleet.

"Earl Howe, as you will remember, was at this time in Chesapeake Bay with a number of British vessels of war. As we have just been doing, he sailed down the one bay and up into the other, but was prevented, by these fortifications of the Americans, from continuing on up the Delaware River to Philadelphia.

"Among his vessels was one called the *Roebuck*, commanded by a Captain Hammond. That officer offered to take upon himself the task of opening a passage for their vessels through the *chevaux-de-frise*, if Howe would send a sufficient force to reduce the fortifications at Billingsport.

"Howe was pleased with the proposition, and two regiments of troops were sent from Chester to accomplish the work. They were successful, made a furious and unexpected assault upon the unfinished works, and the Americans spiked their cannon, set fire to the barracks, and fled. The English demolished the works on the river front, and Hammond, with some difficulty, made a passage way seven feet wide in the *chevaux-de-frise*, so that six of the British vessels passed through and anchored near Hog Island."

"Did they immediately attack Forts Mifflin and Mercer, papa?" asked Lulu.

"It took some little time to make the needed preparations," replied the captain. "It was on the twenty-first of October that Count Donop with twelve hundred picked Hessians crossed the Delaware at Cooper's Ferry and marched to the attack of Fort Mercer. The Americans added eight miles to the extent of their march by taking up the bridge over a creek that they must cross, so compelling them to go four miles up the stream to find a ford.

"It was on the morning of the twety-second that they made their appearance, fully armed for battle, on the edge of a wood within cannon shot of Fort Mercer.

"It was a great surprise to our men, for they had not heard of the approach of these troops. They were informed that there were twenty-five hundred of the Hessians, while they themselves there were but four hundred men in a feeble earth fort with but fourteen pieces of cannon.

"But the brave fellows had no idea of surrendering without a struggle. There were two Rhode Island regiments, commanded by Colonel Christopher Greene. They at once made preparations for defense, and while they were thus engaged a Hessian officer rode up to the fort with a flag and a drummer, and insolently proclaimed, 'The King of England orders his rebellious subjects to lay down their arms; and they were warned that if they stand the battle, no quarter whatever will be given.'

"Colonel Greene answered him, 'We ask no quarter nor will we give any.'

"The Hessian and his drummer then rode hastily back to his commander, and the Hessians at once fell to work building a battery within half cannon shot of the fort.

"At the same time the Americans continued their preparations for the coming conflict, making them with the greatest activity and eagerness, feeling that with them skill and bravery must now combat overwhelming numbers, fierceness, and discipline.

"Their outworks were unfinished but they placed great reliance upon the redoubt.

"At four o'clock in the afternoon the Hessians opened a brisk cannonade, and at a quarter before five a battalion advanced to the attack on the north side of the fort, near a morass which covered it.

"They found there abandoned but not destroyed, and thought they had frightened the Americans away. So with a shout of victory and the drummer beating a lively march, they rushed to the redoubt, where not a man was to be seen.

"But as they reached it and were about to climb the ramparts to plant their flag there, a sudden and galling fire of musketry and grape shot poured out upon them from a half-masked battery on their left flank, formed by an angle of an old embankment.

"It took terrible effect and drove them back to their old entrenchments.

"At the same time another division, commanded by Count Donop himself, attacked the fort on the south side, but they were also driven back with great loss by the continuous and heavy fire of the Americans.

"The fight was a short one but very severe. Donop had fallen, mortally wounded, at the first fire. Mingerode, his second in command, was wounded also, and in all, the enemy left behind in the hasty retreat which followed some four hundred killed and wounded.

"The American galleys and floating batteries in the river galled them considerably in their retreat.

"After the fight was over Manduit, the French engineer who had directed the artillery fire of the fort, was out with a detachment examining and restoring the palisades, when he heard a voice coming from among the killed and wounded of the enemy, saying, 'Whoever you are, draw me hence.'

"It was Count Donop, and Manduit had him carried first into the fort, afterward to a house close at hand occupied by a family named Whitall, where he died three days afterward.

"Donop was but thirty-seven. He said to Manduit, who attended him till he died, 'It is finishing a noble career early; but I die the victim of my ambition and the avarice of my sovereign.'"

"His sovereign? That was George the Third, papa?" Gracie said inquiringly.

"No, Donop was a Hessian, hired out to the British king by his sovereign," replied her father.

"And avarice means love of money?"

"Yes, daughter. And it was avarice on the part of both sovereigns that led to the hiring of the Hessians. The war was waged by the king of England because the Americans refused to be taxed by him at his pleasure and without their consent. He wanted their money.

"Whitall's house, a two-story brick built in 1748, stood close to the river," continued the captain. "I suppose it is still there; it was in 1831, when Lossing visited the locality.

"The Whitalls were Quakers and took no part in the war. When the fort was attacked Mrs. Whitall was urged to flee to some place of safety but declined to do so, saying, 'God's arm is strong, and will protect me; I may do good by staying.'

"She was left alone in the house, and, while the battle was raging, sat in a room in the second story busily at work at her spinning wheel, while the shot came dashing like hail against the walls. At length, a twelve-pound ball from a British vessel in the river just grazed the walnut tree at the fort, which the Americans used as flag staff, crashed into her house through the heavy brick wall on the north gable, then through a partition at the head of the stairs, crossed a recess, and lodged in another partition near where she was sitting.

"At that she gathered up her work and went down to the cellar.

"At the close of the battle the wounded and dying were brought to her house, and she left her work to wait upon them and do all in her power to relieve their sufferings.

"She attended to all, friend and foe, with equal kindness, but scolded the Hessians for coming to America to butcher the people."

"I am sure she must have been a good woman," remarked Gracie. "Oh, I don't know how she could dare to stay in the house while those dreadful balls were flying about it."

"No doubt she felt she was doing her duty," replied the captain. "The path of duty is the safe one. She seems to have been a good Christian woman."

"Yes, indeed!" said Evelyn. "Captain, did not the British attack Fort Mifflin at the same time that the fight was in progress at Fort Mercer?"

"Yes. The firing of the first gun from the Hessian battery was the signal for the British vessels in the river to begin the assault upon the other fort on its opposite side.

"The *Augusta* and several smaller vessels had made their way through the passage in the *chevaux-de-frise* that Hammond had opened, and they were now anchored above it, waiting for flood tide.

"The *Augusta* was a sixty-four gun ship; besides there were the *Merlin,* of eighteen guns; the *Roebuck,* of forty-four; two frigates; and a galley. All these came up with the purpose to attack the fort, but they were kept at bay by the American galleys and floating batteries, which also did good service by flanking the enemy in their attack upon Fort Mercer.

"The British deferred their attack upon Fort Mifflin until the next morning, when, the Hessians having been driven off from Fort Mercer, the American flotilla was able to turn its attention entirely upon the British fleet, which now opened a heavy cannonade upon Fort Mifflin, attempting also to get floating batteries into the channel back of the island.

"But Lieutenant-Colonel Smith, a gallant officer in command of the fort, very vigilant and brave, thwarted all their efforts and greatly assisted the flotilla in repulsing them.

"The fire of the Americans was so fierce and incessant that the British vessels presently tried to fall down the stream to get beyond its reach. But a hot shot struck the *Augusta* and set her on fire. She also got aground on a mud bank near the Jersey shore and at noon blew up.

"The fight between the other British and American vessels went on until three o'clock in the afternoon, when the *Merlin* took fire and blew up near the mouth of Mud Creek.

"The *Roebuck* then dropped down the river below the *chevaux-de-frise*, and for a short time the Americans were left in undisturbed possession of their forts.

"Howe was, however, very anxious to dislodge them, because the river was the only avenue by which provisions could be brought to his army now in Philadelphia.

"On the first of November he took possession of Province Island, lying between Fort Mifflin and the mainland, and began throwing up works to strengthen himself and annoy the defenders of the fort.

"But they showed themselves wonderfully brave and patient. Lieutenant-Colonel Smith was as fine an officer as one could desire to see.

"The principal fortification of Fort Mifflin was in front, that being the side from which vessels coming up the river must be repelled. But on the side toward Province Island it was defended by only a wet ditch. There was a block house at each of its angles, but they were not strong, and when the Americans saw the British take possession of Province Island and began building batteries there, they felt that unless assistance should be sent to dislodge the enemy, the fort would soon be demolished or fall into his possession."

"But couldn't Washington help them, and didn't he try to?" asked Gracie.

"Washington was most desirous to do so and made every effort in his power," replied her father. "If Gates had done his duty, the fort might probably have been saved. Burgoyne's army had been defeated and captured some time before this, and there was then no other formidable enemy in that quarter. But Gates was jealous of Washington and, rather than have him successful, preferred to sacrifice the cause that he had engaged to defend.

"He had ample stores and a formidable force, and had he come promptly to the rescue might have rendered such assistance as to enable Washington to drive the British from Philadelphia and save the forts upon the Delaware.

"But, actuated by the meanest sort of jealousy, he delayed and would not even return Morgan's corps, which Washington had been ill able to spare him.

"Hamilton, sent by Washington to hasten Gates's movements in the matter, grew very indignant at the slow and reluctant compliance of Gates, and by plainly expressing his opinion induced him to send a stronger reinforcement than he had intended.

"Putnam also made trouble by detaining some of the troops forwarded by Gates to assist him in carrying out a plan of his own for attacking New York.

"Governor Clinton then advised Hamilton to issue a peremptory order to Putnam to set those troops in motion for Whitemarsh where Washington was encamped. Hamilton did so, and the troops were sent."

"Dear, dear!" sighed Lulu. "What a time poor Washington did have with Congress being so slow and officers under him so perverse, wanting their own way instead of doing their best to help him to carry out his good and wise plans."

"Yes," her father said with a slight twinkle of fun in his eye. "But doesn't my eldest daughter feel something like sympathy with them in their wish to carry out their own plans without much regard for those of other people?"

"I—I suppose perhaps I ought to, papa," she replied, blushing and hanging her head rather shamefacedly. "And yet," she added, lifting it again and smiling up into his eyes, "I do think if you had been the commander over me I'd have tried to follow your directions, believing you knew better than I."

She moved nearer to his side and leaned up lovingly against him as she spoke.

"Yes, dear child, I feel quite sure of it," he returned, laying his hand tenderly on her head then smoothing her hair caressingly as he spoke.

"But you haven't finished about the second attack upon Fort Mifflin have you, brother Levis?" queried Walter.

"No, not quite," the captain answered, then went on with his narrative.

"All through the war Washington showed himself wonderfully patient and hopeful, but it was with intense anxiety he now watched the progress of the enemy in his designs upon Fort Mifflin, unable as he himself was to succor its threatened garrison."

"But why couldn't he go and help them with his soldiers, papa?" asked Gracie.

"Because, daughter, if he broke up his camp at Whitemarsh and moved his army to the other side of the Schuylkill, he must leave stores and hospitals for the sick within reach of the enemy; leave the British troops in possession of the fords of the river; make it difficult, if not impossible, for the troops he was expecting from the North to join him, and perhaps bring on a battle while he was too weak to hope for victory over such odds as Howe could bring against him.

"So the poor fellows in the fort had to fight it out themselves with no assistance from outside."

"Couldn't they have slipped out in the night and gone quietly without fighting, papa?" asked Gracie.

"Perhaps so," he said with a slight smile. "But such doings as that would never have helped our country to free herself from the British yoke, and these men were too brave and patriotic to try it. They were freemen and never could be slaves. To them death was preferable to slavery. We may well be proud of the skill and courage with which Lieutenant-Colonel Smith defended his fort against the foe.

"On the tenth of November the British opened their batteries on land and water. They had five on Province Island within five hundred yards of the fort; a large floating battery with twenty-two twenty-four pounders, which they brought up within forty yards of an angle of the fort; also six ships, two of them with forty guns each, all within less than nine hundred yards of the fort."

"More than three hundred guns all firing on that one little fort!" exclaimed Rosie. "It is really wonderful how our poor men could stand it."

"Yes, for six consecutive days a perfect storm of bombs and round shot poured upon them," said the captain. "And it must have required no small amount of courage to stand such a tempest."

"I hope they fired back and killed some of those wicked fellows!" exclaimed Walter, his eyes flashing.

"You may be sure they did their best to defend themselves and their fort," replied the captain.

"And the British loss was great, though the exact number has never been known.

"Nearly two hundred and fifty of our men were killed or wounded. Lieutenant Treat, commanding the artillery, was killed on the first day by the bursting of a bomb. The next day quite a number of the garrison were killed or wounded, and Colonel Smith himself had a narrow escape.

"A ball passed through a chimney in the barracks, wither he had gone intending to write a letter, scattered the bricks, one of them striking him on the head knocking him senseless.

"He was carried across the river to Red Bank, and Major Thayer of the Rhode Island line took command in his place.

"The first day a battery of two guns was destroyed, a blockhouse and the laboratory were blown up, and the garrison were compelled to keep within the fort. All that night the British threw shells, and the scene was a terrible one indeed, especially for the poor fellows inside the fort.

"The next morning, about sunrise, they saw thirty armed boats coming against them. That night the heavy floating battery was brought to bear upon the fort. The next morning it opened with terrible effect, yet they endured it, and made the enemy suffer so much from their fire that they began to think seriously of giving up the contest. Then one of the men in the fort deserted them, and his tale of the weakness of the garrison inspiring the British with renewed hope of conquest, they prepared for a more general and vigorous assault.

"At daylight on the fifteenth two men-of-war, the *Iris* and the *Somerset*, passed up the channel in front of the fort on Mud Island. Two others—the *Vigilant* and a hulk with three twenty-four pounders—passed through the narrow channel on the west side and were placed in a position to act in concert with the batteries of Province Island in enfilading the American works.

"At ten o'clock all was silent, and doubtless our men were awaiting the coming onslaught with intense anxiety, when a signal bugle sounded and instantly all the ships and batteries poured a storm of shot and shell from the mouths of their many guns upon the devoted little garrison."

"Oh, how dreadful!" sighed Gracie. "Could they stand it, papa?"

"They endured it with astonishing courage," replied the captain. "While all day long, and far into the evening, it was kept up without cessation. The yards of the British ships hung nearly over the American battery, and there were musketeers stationed in their tops who immediately shot down every man who showed himself on the platform of the fort. Our men displayed, as I have said, wonderful bravery and endurance. There seems to have been no thought of surrender, but long before night palisades, blockhouses, parapet, embrasures—all were ruined.

"Early in the evening Major Thayer sent all but forty of his men to Red Bank. He and the remaining forty stayed on in the fort until midnight, then, setting fire to the remains of the barracks, they also escaped in safety to Red Bank.

"Lossing tells us that in the course of that last day more than a thousand discharges of cannon, from twelve- to thirty-two pounders, were made against the works on Mud Island, and that it was one of the most gallant and obstinate defenses of the war.

"Major Thayer received great credit for his share in it and was presented with a sword by the Rhode Island Assembly as a token of their appreciation of his services there."

"Did not Captain—afterward Commodore—Talbot do himself great credit there?" asked Evelyn.

"Yes. He fought for hours with his wrist shattered by a musket ball, then he was wounded in the hip and was sent to Red Bank. He was a very brave man and did much good service during the war, principally on the water, taking vessel after vessel. In the fight with one of them—the *Dragon*—his speaking trumpet was pierced by bullets, and the skirts of his coat were shot away."

"How brave he must have been!" exclaimed Lulu with enthusiasm. "Don't you think so, papa?"

"Indeed, I do," replied the captain. "He was only one of the many men of that period of whom their countrymen may be justly proud."

※※※※※※※※※

CHAPTER FIFTH

LITTLE NED, WHO was not very well, began fretting and reaching out his arms to be taken by his father. The captain lifted him tenderly, saying something in a soothing tone, and carried him to another part of the deck.

Then the young people, gathering about Grandma Elsie, who had been an almost silent listener to Captain Raymond's account of the attacks upon the forts and the gallant conduct of their defenders, begged her to tell them something more of the stirring events of those revolutionary days.

"You have visited the places near here where there was fighting in those days, haven't you, mamma?" asked Walter.

"Yes, some years ago," she replied. "Ah, how many years ago was it?" she added musingly, then continued. "When I was quite a little girl, my father took me to Philadelphia and a number of other places, where occurred notable events in the war of the Revolution."

"And you will tell us about them, won't you, mamma?" Walter asked in coaxing tones.

"Certainly, if you and the rest all wish it," she returned, smiling lovingly into the eager young faces, while the others joined in the request.

"Please tell about Philadelphia first, mamma," Walter went on. "You went to Independence Hall, of course, and we've all been there, I believe. But there must be some other points of interest in and about the city, I should think, that will be rather new to us."

"Yes, there are others," she replied. "Though I suppose that to every American, Independence Hall is the most interesting of all, since it was there the Continental Congress held its meetings, and its bell that proclaimed the glad tidings that that grand Declaration of Independence had been signed and the colonies of Great Britain had become free and independent states—though there was long and desperate fighting to go through before England would acknowledge it."

"Mamma, don't you hate old England for it?" cried Walter impulsively, his eyes flashing.

"No, indeed!" she replied, laughing softly and patting his rosy cheek with her still pretty white hand. "It was not the England of today, you must remember, my son, nor indeed the England of that day, but her half crazy king and his ministers, who thought to raise money for him by unjust taxation of the people of this land. 'Taxation without representation is tyranny.' So they felt and said, and as such resisted it."

"And I'm proud of them for doing so!" he exclaimed, his eyes sparkling. "Now, what other Revolutionary places are to be seen in Philadelphia, mamma dear?"

"There is Christ Church, where Washington, Franklin, members of Congress, and officers of the Continental army used to worship; its grave-yard where Franklin and his wife, Deborah, lie buried. Major-General Lee, too, was laid there; also General Mercer, killed at the battle of Princeton, was originally laid there, but his body was afterward removed to Laurel Hill Cemetery."

"We will visit Christ Church, I hope," said Rosie. "Carpenter's Hall, too, where the first Continental Congress met, and Loxley House, where Lydia Darrah lived in Revolutionary times. You saw that, I suppose, mamma?"

"Yes," replied her mother. "But I do not know whether it is, or is not, still standing."

"That's a nice story about Lydia Darrah," remarked Walter with satisfaction. "I think she showed herself a grand woman. Don't you, mamma?"

"I do, indeed," replied his mother. "She was a true patriot."

"There were many grand men and women in our country in those times," remarked Evelyn Leland. "The members of that first Congress that met in Carpenter's Hall on Monday, the fifth of September, 1774, were such. Do you not think so, Grandma Elsie?"

"Yes, I quite agree with you," replied Mrs. Travilla. "It was John Adams—himself by no means one of the least—who said, 'There is in the Congress a collection of the greatest men upon the continent in point of abilities, virtues, and fortunes.'"

"Washington was one of them, wasn't he, Grandma Elsie?" asked Lulu.

"Yes, one of the members from Virginia. The others from that state were Richard Henry Lee, Peyton Randolph, Richard Bland, Benjamin Harrison, Edmund Pendleton, and Patrick Henry. Peyton Randolph was chosen president, and Charles Thomson, of Pennsylvania, secretary."

"I suppose, they set to work on fighting the tyranny of George the Third," commented Lulu.

"Lossing tells us," replied Mrs. Travilla, "that the delegates from the different colonies then presented their credentials, and after that there was silence, while deep anxiety was depicted on every countenance. It seemed difficult to know how to begin upon the work for which they had been called together. But at length a grave-looking member, in a plain suit of gray and wearing an unpowdered wig, arose. So plain was his appearance that Bishop White, who was present, afterward telling of the circumstances, said he 'felt a regret that a seeming country parson should so far have mistaken his talents and the theater for their display.' However, he soon changed his mind as the plain-looking man began to speak. His words were so eloquent, his sentiments so logical, his voice was so musical, that the whole House was electrified, while from lip to lip ran the question, 'Who is he? Who is he?' and the few who knew the stranger answered, 'It is Patrick Henry of Virginia.'"

"Oh, mamma, was it before that that he had said, 'Give me liberty or give me death'?" queried Walter, his eyes sparkling with enthusiasm.

"No, he said that a few months afterward. But about nine years before, he had startled his hearers in the Virginia House of Burgesses by his cry, 'Caesar had his Brutus, Charles the First his Cromwell, and George the Third may profit by their example'!"

"Now he was starting the Congress at its work!"

"You are right. There was no more hesitation. They arranged their business, adopted rules for the regulation of their sessions, and then—at the beginning of the third day, when about to enter upon the business that had called them together—Mr.

Cushing moved that the sessions should be opened with prayer for Divine guidance and aid.

"Mr. John Adams, in a letter to his wife, written the next day, said that Mr. Cushing's motion was opposed by a member from New York and one from South Carolina, because the assembly was composed of men of so many different denominations—Congregationalists, Presbyterians, Quakers, Anabaptists, and Episcopalians—that they could not join in the same act of worship.

"Then Mr. Samuel Adams arose and said that he was no bigot and could hear a prayer from any gentleman of piety and virtue who was at the same time a friend of his country. He was a stranger in Philadelphia, but he had heard that Mr. Duche deserved that character, so he moved that he—Mr. Duche, an Episcopal clergyman—be desired to read prayers before the Congress the next morning.

"Mr. Duche consented, and the next morning read the prayers and the Psalter for the seventh of September. A part of it was the thirty-fifth Psalm, which seemed wonderfully appropriate. Do you remember how it begins? 'Plead my cause, O Lord, with them that strive with me: fight against them that fight against me. Take hold of shield and buckler, and stand up for mine help.'"

"It does seem wonderfully appropriate," said Evelyn. "Oh, I'm sure that God was on the side of the patriots and helped them greatly in their hard struggle with their powerful foe!"

"Yes, only by His all-powerful aid could our liberties have been won, and to Him be all the glory and praise," said Grandma Elsie, gratitude and joy shining in her beautiful eyes.

"But that wasn't the Congress that signed the Declaration?" Walter asked.

"No, this was in 1774, and the Declaration was not signed until July, 1776," replied his mother.

"It seems to me," remarked Lulu, "that the Americans were very slow in saying they would be free from England—free from British tyranny."

"But you know you're always in a great hurry to do things, Lu," put in Gracie softly with an affectionate, admiring smile up into her sister's face.

"Yes, I believe you're right, Gracie," returned Lulu with a pleased laugh, giving Gracie's hand a loving squeeze.

"Yes," assented Grandma Elsie, "our people were slow to break with the mother country—as they used to call old England, the land of their ancestors. They bore long and patiently with her, but at last were convinced that in that case patience had ceased to be a virtue, and liberty for themselves and their children must be secured at all costs."

"How soon were they convinced of it, mamma?" asked Walter.

"The conviction came slowly to all, and to some more slowly than others," she replied. "Dr. Franklin, Samuel Adams, and Patrick Henry were among the first to see the necessity of becoming, politically, entirely free and independent.

"It is stated on good authority that Patrick Henry in speaking of Great Britain, as early as 1773, said, 'She will drive us to extremities; no accommodation will take place; hostilities will soon commence, and a desperate and bloody touch it will be.'

"Someone, present when the remark was made, asked Mr. Henry if he thought the colonies strong enough to resist successfully the fleets and armies of Great Britain, and he answered that he doubted whether they would be able to do so alone, 'but that France, Spain, and Holland were the natural enemies of Great Britain.'

"'Where will they be all this while?' he asked. 'Do you suppose they will stand by, idle and indifferent spectators to the contest? Will Louis XVI be asleep all this time? Believe me, no! When Louis XVI shall be satisfied by our serious opposition and our Declaration of Independence, that all prospect of a reconciliation is gone, then, and not till then, will he furnish us with arms, ammunition, and clothing; and not with them only, but he will send his fleets and armies to fight our battles for us; he will form a treaty with us, offensive and defensive, against our unnatural mother. Spain and Holland will join the confederation! Our independence will be established! And we shall take our stand among the nations of the earth!'"

"And it all happened so; didn't it, mamma?" exclaimed Rosie exultantly. "Just as Patrick Henry had predicted."

"Yes," replied her mother with a proud and happy smile. "We have certainly taken our place — by God's blessing upon the efforts of those brave and gallant heroes of the Revolution — as one of the greatest nations of the earth.

"Yet not all the credit should be awarded them, but some of it given to their successors in the nation's counsels and on the fields of battle. The foundations were well and strongly laid by our revolutionary fathers, and the work well carried on by their successors."

"Grandma Elsie, what was the story about Lydia Darrah?" asked Gracie. "I don't remember to have heard it."

"She lived in Philadelphia when the British were in possession of the city there during the winter after the battle of Brandywine," replied Mrs. Travilla. "She belonged to the Society of Friends, most of whom, as you doubtless remember, took no active part in the war. At least, they did none of the fighting, though many helped in other ways. But some were Tories, who gave aid and comfort to the enemy in other ways than by the use of arms."

"What a shame!" cried Walter. "You will tell us about the doings of some of those when you are done with the story of Lydia Darrah, won't you, mamma?"

"If you all wish it," she answered. She then went on with her narrative.

"Judging from her conduct at the time, Lydia must have been an ardent patriot, but patriots and Tories alike had British officers quartered upon them. The adjutant-general took up his quarters in Loxley House, the home of the Darrahs, and, as it was a secluded place, the superior officers frequently held meetings there for private conferences on matters connected with the movements of the British troops.

"One day the adjutant-general told Mrs. Darrah that such a meeting was to be held that evening, and that he wanted the upper back room made ready for himself and the friends who would be present. He added that they would be likely to stay late, and she must be sure to see that all her family were early in their beds.

"His tone and manner led Mrs. Darrah to think something of importance was going forward, and though she did not dare disobey his order, she resolved to try to find out what was their object in holding this private night meeting. She was probably hoping to be able to do something to prevent the carrying out of their plans against the liberties of her country.

"She sent her family to bed early, according to directions, before the officers came, and after admitting them, she retired to her own couch. But she was not to sleep, for her thoughts were busy with conjectures in regard to the mischief they — the unwelcome intruders in her house — might be plotting against her country.

"She had lain down without undressing, and after a little she rose and stole softly, in her stocking feet, to the door of the room where they were assembled.

"All was quiet at the moment when she reached it. She put her ear to the keyhole and — doubtless with a fast-beating heart — waited there, listening intently for the sound of the officers' voices.

"For a few minutes all was silence. Then it was broken by a single voice reading aloud an order from Sir William Howe for the troops to march out of the city the next night and make an attack upon Washington's camp at Whitemarsh.

"Lydia waited to hear no more, for that information was sufficient. It would have been dangerous indeed for her to be caught there.

"She hastened back to her own room and again threw herself on the bed, but not to sleep, as you may well imagine.

"Presently the opening and shutting of doors told her that the visitors of the adjutant-general were taking their departure. There was a rap on her door, but she did not answer it. It was repeated, but still she did not move or speak. At the third knock she rose, went to the door, and found the adjutant-general there.

"He informed her that his friends had gone, and she might close her house for the night.

"She did so, then lay down again, but not to sleep. She lay thinking of the momentous secret she had just learned, considering how she might help to avert the threatened danger to the patriot army and asking help and guidance from her heavenly Father.

"Her prayer was heard. She laid her plans, then at early dawn, arose. Waking her husband, she told him flour was wanted for the family and she must go immediately to the mill at Frankford for it. Then taking a bag to carry it in, she started at once on foot.

"At General Howe's headquarters she obtained a passport to leave the city.

"She had a five miles' walk to Frankford, where she left her bag at the mill and hurried on toward the American camp to deliver her tidings.

"It was still quite early, but before reaching the camp, she met an American officer, Lieutenant Craig, whom Washington had sent out to seek information in regard to the doings of the enemy.

"Lydia quickly told him her story then hastened back to the mill for her bag of flour and hurried home with it."

"Mamma," exclaimed Walter, "how could she carry anything so big and heavy?"

"Perhaps it was but a small bag," returned her mother with a smile. "I never saw or read any statement as to its size. Perhaps the joy and thankfulness she felt in having been permitted and enabled to do such service to the cause of her country may have helped to strengthen her to bear her heavy burden."

"What a day it must have been to her!" exclaimed Evelyn. "Hope and fear alternating in her heart. How her heart must have gone up constantly in prayer to God for His blessing upon her poor, bleeding country."

"And how it must have throbbed with alternating hope and fear as she stood at the window that cold, starry night and watched the departure of the British troops to make the intended attack upon Washington and his little army," said Rosie. "And again when the distant roll of a drum told that they were returning."

"Yes," said Lulu. "And when the adjutant-general came back to the house, summoned Lydia to his room, and shut her in there and locked the door."

"Oh," cried Gracie, "did he know it was she that had told of his plans?"

"No," said Mrs. Travilla. "From the accounts I have read he does not seem to have even suspected her. He invited her to be seated, then asked, 'Were any of your family up, Lydia, on the night when I received company in this house?' 'No,' she replied. 'They all retired at eight o'clock.' 'It is strange,' he returned. 'You, I know, were asleep, for I knocked at your door three times before you heard me, yet it is certain we were betrayed. I am altogether at a loss to conceive who could have given information to Washington of our intended attack. On arriving near his camp, we found his cannon mounted, his troops under arms, and so prepared at every point to receive us, that we have been compelled to march back like a parcel of fools, without injury to our enemy!'"

"I hope the British did not find out, before they left Philadelphia, who had given the information to the Americans and take vengeance on her," said Walter.

"No," replied his mother. "Fearing that, she begged Lieutenant Craig to keep her secret, which he did. It has so happened that her good deed finds no mention in the histories of that time and is recorded only by well-authenticated tradition."

"So all the Quakers were not Tories?" remarked Walter in a satisfied yet half inquiring tone.

"Oh, no, indeed!" replied his mother. "There were ardent patriots among them, as among people of other denominations. Nathanael Greene—after Washington, one of our best and greatest generals— was of a Quaker family, and I have heard that when his mother found he was not to be persuaded to refrain from taking an active part in the struggle for freedom, she said to him, 'Well, Nathanael, if thee must fight, let me never hear of thee having a wound in thy back!'"

"Ah, she must have been brave and patriotic," laughed Walter. "I doubt if she was so very sorry that her son was determined to fight for the freedom of his country."

"No," said Rosie, "I don't believe she was, and I don't see how she could help feeling proud of him—so bright, brave, talented, and patriotic as he showed himself to be all through the war."

"Yes," said Lulu. "I don't think he has half the honors he deserved, though at West Point we saw a cannon with an inscription on it saying it had been taken from the British army and presented by Congress to Major-General Greene as a monument of their high sense of his service in the Revolutionary War."

"Weren't the Tories very bad men, Grandma Elsie?" asked Gracie.

"Not all of them, my dear," replied Mrs. Travilla, smiling lovingly into the sweet, though grave and earnest, little face. "Some were really conscientiously opposed to war, even when waged for freedom from unbearable tyranny and oppression. But they were disposed to be merely inactive witnesses of the struggle, some of them desiring the success of the patriots, other's that of the king's troops. Then there was another set who, while professing neutrality, secretly aided the British, betraying the patriots into their hands.

"Such were Carlisle and Roberts, Quakers of that time, living in Philadelphia. While the British were in possession of the city those two men were employed as secret agents in detecting foes to the government. By their secret information, they caused many patriots to be arrested and thrown into prison. Lossing tells us that Carlisle, wearing the meek garb and deportment of a Quaker, was at heart a Torquemada."

"And who was Torquemada, mamma?" queried Walter softly.

"A Dominican monk of Spain, who lived in the times of Ferdinand and Isabella, and was by them appointed inquisitor-general. He organized the Inquisition throughout Spain, drew up the code of procedure, and during sixteen years caused between nine and ten thousand persons to be burned at the stake."

"Mamma! What a cruel, cruel wretch!" cried Walter. "Oh, but I'm glad nobody can do such cruel things in these days! I hope Roberts and Carlisle weren't quite as wicked as he."

"No, I should not like to think they would have been willing to go to quite such lengths, though they seem to have shown enough malignity toward their patriotic fellow countrymen to make it evident that they had something of the spirit of the cruel and bloodthirsty Torquemada.

"Though they would not bears arms for the wealth of the Indies, they were ever ready to act as guides to those whose object was to massacre their fellow countrymen, and that only because they were determined to be free."

"Were not some of those in New Jersey known as 'Pine Robbers,' Grandma Elsie?" asked Evelyn.

"Yes. They infested the lower part of Monmouth County, whence they went on predatory excursions into other parts of the state, coming upon people at night to burn, murder, plunder, and destroy. They burrowed caves in the sand hills on the borders of the swamps, where they concealed themselves and their booty."

"Did they leave their hiding places only in the night time, mamma?" asked Walter.

"No," she replied. "They would sometimes sally forth during the day and attack the farmers in their fields. So that the men were compelled to carry muskets and be ready to fight for their lives, while women and children were kept in a constant state of terror."

"I think I have read that one of the worst of them was a blacksmith living in Freehold?" remarked Evelyn in her quiet way.

"Yes, his name was Fenton. He was a very wicked man, who, like many others calling themselves Tories, took advantage of the disturbance of the times to rob and murder his fellow countrymen. He began his career of robbery and murder very early in the war.

"One of his first acts, as such, was the plundering of a tailor's shop in the township. A committee of vigilance had been already organized, and its members sent Fenton word that if he did not return what he had stolen he should be hunted out and shot.

"He was a coward, as such villains almost always are, and did return the clothing, sending with it a written message, 'I have returned your — — — rags. In a short time I am coming to burn your barns and houses and roast you all like a pack of kittens.'

"One summer night, shortly afterward, he led a gang of desperadoes like himself against the dwelling of an old man named Farr. There were but three persons in the house—the old man, his wife, and daughter. They barricaded their door and defended themselves for a while, but Fenton broke in a part of the door, fired through the hole at the old man and broke his leg. The women could not keep them out much longer; they soon forced an entrance, murdered the old man and woman, and badly wounded the daughter. She, however, made her escape, and the cowardly ruffians fled without waiting to secure their plunder—no doubt fearing she would bring a band of patriots to avenge the slain."

"I hope that wretch, Fenton, was soon caught and well punished for his robberies and murders!" exclaimed Lulu.

"He was," replied Grandma Elsie. "The Bible tells us the 'bloody and deceitful men shall not live out half their days,' and Fenton's fate was one amongst many to prove the truth of it.

"He had met a young man on his way to mill, plundering and beating him. The victim carried his complaint to Lee, and a sergeant and two soldiers were detailed to capture or kill Fenton.

"They used strategy with success. The two soldiers were secreted under some straw in the bottom of a wagon, the sergeant disguised himself as a country-man, and the young man took a seat in the vehicle. Then they drove on toward the mill, expecting to meet Fenton on the road. They were passing a low groggery among the pines, when he came out of it, pistol in hand, and impudently ordered them to stop.

"They drew rein, and he came nearer, asking if they had any brandy with them. They replied that they had and handed him a bottle. Then, as he lifted it to his lips, the sergeant silently signaled to one of the hidden soldiers, who at once rose from his hiding place in the straw and shot Fenton through the head. His body was then thrown into the wagon and carried in triumph to Freehold."

"The people of that part of the country must have felt a good deal relieved," remarked Rosie. "Still there were Fenton's desperado companions left."

"Two of them—Fagan and West—shared Fenton's fate, being shot by the exasperated people," said her mother. "West's body was hung in chains with hoop iron bands around it on a chestnut tree hard by the roadside, about a mile from Freehold."

"Oh, Grandma Elsie, is it there yet?" asked Gracie, shuddering with horror.

"No, dear child, that could hardly be possible after so many years—more than a hundred you will remember when you think of it," returned Mrs. Travilla with a kindly reassuring smile.

"I hope papa will take us to Freehold," said Lulu. "I want to see the battleground."

"I feel quite sure he will, should nothing happen to prevent," said Grandma Elsie.

"Wasn't it at Freehold, or in its neighborhood that a Captain Huddy was murdered by those very same 'Pine Robbers'?" asked Evelyn.

"Yes," replied Grandma Elsie. "It was only the other day that I was refreshing my memory in regard to it by glancing over Lossing's account given in his *Field Book of the Revolution*."

"Please tell us about it, mamma," pleaded Walter.

"Very willingly, since you wish to hear it," she said, noting the look of eager interest on the young faces about her.

"Captain Huddy was a very ardent patriot and consequently hated by his Tory neighbors. He lived at a place called Colt's Neck, about five miles away from Freehold.

"One evening, in the summer of 1780, a party of some sixty refugees, headed by a mulatto named Titus, attacked Huddy's house. There was no one in it at the time but Huddy himself and a servant girl, some twenty years old, named Lucretia Emmons."

"She wouldn't be of much use fighting men," remarked Walter with a slight sniff of contempt.

"Perhaps Captain Huddy thought differently," replied his mother with a slightly amused smile. "There were several guns in the house, which she loaded for Huddy while he passed from one window to another firing through them at his foes. Titus and several others were wounded, and then they set fire to the house and Huddy surrendered.

"He was taken on board a boat from which he jumped into the water and escaped, assisted in so doing by the fire of some militia who were in pursuit of the Tories.

"About two years later Huddy was in command of a block house near the village of Tom's River, when it was attacked by some refugees from New York, and, his ammunition giving out, he was obliged to surrender. He and his companions were taken to New York, then back to Sandy Hook, where they were placed on board a guard-ship and heavily ironed.

"Shortly afterward he was taken to Gravelly Point by sixteen refugees under Captain Lippincott and hung on a gallows made of three rails.

"He met his fate like the brave man that he was, calmly writing his will on the head of the barrel upon which he was to stand for execution.

"A desperate Tory named Philip White had been killed while Huddy was a prisoner in New York, and these men falsely accused Huddy of having a share in his death. After hanging him, that cruel, wicked Lippincott fastened to his chest a notice to the effect that they had killed Captain Huddy in revenge for the death of Philip White, and that they were determined to hang man for man while a refugee lived."

"Oh, what dreadful things people did in those days!" sighed Gracie. "Did anybody venture to take the body down and bury it, Grandma Elsie?"

"Yes. Captain Huddy's body was carried to Freehold and buried with the honors of war."

"And did the people care much about it?"

"Yes, indeed! His death caused great excitement and indignation, and Dr. Woodhull, the Freehold minister, who preached the funeral sermon from the piazza of the hotel, earnestly entreated Washington to retaliate in order to prevent a repetition of such deeds.

"Washington consented, but, ever merciful, first wrote to Sir Henry Clinton that unless the murderers of Captain Huddy were given up he should retaliate.

"Clinton refused, and a young British officer, Captain Asgill, a prisoner in the hands of the Americans, was selected by lot for execution. Washington, however, mercifully postponed the carrying out of the sentence, feeling much pity and sympathy for the young man and doubtless for his relatives also. Letters came from Europe earnestly entreating that Asgill's life might be spared, among them a pathetic one from his mother and an intercessory one from the French minister, Count de Vergennes.

"These letters Washington sent to Congress and that body passed a resolution, 'That the comman-der-in-chief be, and hereby is, directed to set Captain Asgill at liberty.'"

"It seems to me that our people were far more merciful than the English," remarked Lulu with a look of patriotic pride.

"I think that is true," assented Grandma Elsie. "Not meaning to deny that there are many kind-hearted men among the British of today, or that there were such among them even then, but most of those then in power showed themselves to be avaricious, hardhearted, and cruel."

"Yes, they wanted to make slaves of the people here," exclaimed Lulu hotly. "But they found that Americans wouldn't be slaves—that rather than resign their liberty they would die fighting for it."

CHAPTER SIXTH

IT WAS STILL EARLY in the evening when the *Dolphin* reached her wharf at Philadelphia, where her passengers found friends and relatives waiting to give them a joyous reception.

A few days passed very pleasantly in visiting these friends and places of interest in the city, particularly such as were in one way or another connected with the events of Revolutionary times. Then they went up the Delaware in their yacht.

Their first halting-place would be at Trenton, and naturally the talk, as they went up the river, was largely of the Revolutionary events that had taken place there and at other not far distant points. Grandma Elsie was again the narrator.

"In November of 1776," she began, "our dear country's prospects looked very dark. On the sixteenth, Fort Washington, on the east bank of the Hudson and near New York City, fell into the hands of the enemy, and its garrison of nearly three thousand men were made prisoners of war.

"On the twentieth Cornwallis crossed the Hudson at Dobbs Ferry and with his six thousand men attacked Fort Lee. The garrison hastily retreated, leaving their baggage and military stores, and joined the main army at Hackensack, then five miles away.

"Then Washington, who had with him scarcely three thousand men, began a retreat toward the Delaware, hoping to obtain reinforcements in New Jersey and Pennsylvania that would enable him to make a stand against the invaders and give them battle.

"But his troops had become much dispirited by the many recent disasters to our arms, delayed payment of arrears by Congress, causing them great inconvenience and suffering, lack of proper food and clothing, and the presence of the enemy, who now had possession of New Jersey and seemed likely soon to take Philadelphia.

"Just at that time, as I have said, there seemed little hope for our country. Washington's army was dwindling very rapidly—men whose terms of enlistment had expired were refusing to serve any longer—so that he had but twenty-two hundred under his command when he crossed the Delaware. Two days later he had not more than seventeen hundred—indeed, scarcely more than a thousand on whom he could rely.

"He wrote to General Lee, who had been left at White Plains with nearly three thousand men, asking him to lead his division into New Jersey to reinforce his rapidly melting army. Lee paid no attention to the request, and Washington sent him a positive command to do what he had before requested.

"Lee obeyed very slowly, and while on his way, he was taken prisoner by the enemy."

"Served him right for disobeying Washington!" growled Walter.

"There could be no excuse for such blatant disobedience," continued Grandma Elsie. "And one feels no sympathy for Lee in reading of his sudden seizure by the British, who carried him off in such haste that he had no time to dress but was taken bareheaded and in blanket coat and slippers."

"I doubt if his capture was a loss to the American cause, then," remarked Rosie.

"No," said her mother. "Though much deplored at the time, I have no doubt it was really for the good of the cause. General Sullivan succeeded Lee in command and presently joined Washington with his forces."

"I don't see how Washington could have patience with so many disappointments and delays," said Lulu. "Didn't he ever give way to despair, even for a little while, Grandma Elsie?"

"I have never seen the least intimation of it," replied Mrs. Travilla. "He is said to have been at this time firm, calm, undaunted, holding fast to his faith in the final triumph of the good cause for which he was toiling and striving.

"There seemed to be nothing but the Delaware between the enemy and his conquest of Philadelphia—the freezing of the river so that the British could pass over it on the ice might occur at any time. Someone asked Washington what he would do were Philadelphia to be taken. He answered, 'We will retreat beyond the Susquehanna River, and thence, if necessary, to the Allegheny Mountains.' Doubtless he was even then planning the masterly movements of his forces that presently drove the enemy from Trenton and Princeton."

"Didn't the people of Philadelphia try to be ready to defend themselves and their city, mamma?" asked Walter.

"Yes," she replied. "Congress gave the command there with almost unlimited power to General

Putnam, appointing a committee of three to act for them, they adjourned to reassemble in Baltimore.

"In the meantime Washington was getting ready for the striking of his intended blows in New Jersey.

"It would seem that General Howe, the commander-in-chief of the British forces, had planned to dispatch Cornwallis up the Hudson to the assistance of Burgoyne, who was about to invade our country from Canada. But Cornwallis had a strong desire to capture Philadelphia, and he probably held no doubt that he could do so if allowed to carry out his plans, and to that Howe consented.

"Cornwallis showed little skill in the arrangement of his forces, scattering them here and there in detachments from New Brunswick to the Delaware and down that stream to a point below Burlington. His military stores, and his strongest detachment, were at New Brunswick. The last consisted of a troop of light horse with about fifteen hundred Hessians.

"Washington decided to surprise those troops while at the same time Generals Ewing and Cadwalader with the Pennsylvania militia were directed to attack the posts at Bordentown, Black Horse, Burlington, and Mount Holly. Cadwalader was to cross near Bristol, Ewing below Trenton Falls, while Washington, with Generals Greene and Sullivan and Colonel Knox of the artillery, was to lead the main body of Continental troops and cross the Delaware at M'Conkey's Ferry.

"Washington was very, very anxious to save Philadelphia, which Cornwallis was aiming to capture and felt sure of taking without any great difficulty after crossing the Delaware since he had heard that the people there were for the king almost to a man. So sure was he indeed that the victory would be an easy one that he had gone back to his headquarters in New York and prepared to return to England.

"Putnam who was in Philadelphia, had heard of Washington's intended attack upon the British at Trenton and to assist him sent Colonel Griffin at the head of four hundred and fifty militia across from Philadelphia to New Jersey with directions to make a diversion in favor of the Americans by marching to Mount Holly as if intending an attack upon the British troops under the command of Colonel Donop at Bordentown.

"Donop fell into the trap, moved against Griffin with his whole force of two thousand men, and, as Griffin retreated before him, followed. Then, secure like Cornwallis and other of the English officers in the belief that the Americans were well nigh subdued already, and that when once Philadelphia should fall, resistance would be about at an end, moved his troops in so dilatory a manner that he was two days in returning to his post."

"Humph! They were mightily mistaken in their estimate of our people, weren't they, mamma?" exclaimed Walter.

"I think they were themselves soon convinced of that," she answered with a smile, then continued her story.

"Washington selected Christmas night as the time for his contemplated attack upon the British at Trenton. It was, as he well knew, the habit of the Germans to celebrate that day with feasting and drinking. Such being the case, he felt that he might reasonably expect to find them under the influence of intoxicating drinks, therefore unfit for any kind of successful resistance.

"The river had been free from ice, but in the last twenty-four hours before the appointed time for the expedition, the weather changed. It had grown very much colder so that the water was filled with floating ice, greatly increasing the difficulty and danger of crossing; a storm of sleet and snow set in, too, and the night was dark and gloomy.

"Still the little army was undaunted. They paraded at M'Conkey's Ferry at dusk, expecting to reach Trenton by midnight. But so slow and perilous was the crossing that it was nearly four o'clock when at last they mustered on the Jersey shore.

"It was now too late to attack under cover of the darkness, as had been Washington's plan."

"Excuse me, mamma, but surely it would be still dark at four o'clock in the morning?" Walter said half inquiringly.

"Yes, my son, but you must remember they had crossed at M'Conkey's Ferry, which is eight miles higher up the river than is Trenton, so that they had that distance to march before they could even begin to make their attack.

"Washington divided his forces, leading one portion himself by the upper road—Generals Greene, Mercer, and Lord Sterling accompanying him. He gave Sullivan command of the other, which was to approach the town by another road leading along the river.

"The two arrived at Trenton about the same time, having marched so silently that the enemy was unaware of their approach till they were but a short distance from the picket guards on the outskirts of town.

"There was a brisk skirmish then, the Hessians retreating toward their main body, firing as they went from behind the houses, while the Americans pursued them closely."

"Then the Hessians weren't drunk as Washington expected, were they, Grandma Elsie?" asked Gracie.

"Well-authenticated tradition says they were," replied Mrs. Travilla. "They had been carousing through the night, Rall himself feasting, drinking, and playing cards at the house of Abraham Hunt, who had invited him and other officers to a Christmas supper. They had been playing all night and regaling themselves with wine.

"A Tory on the Pennington Road saw, about dawn, the approach of the Americans under Washington and sent a messenger with a note to warn Rall. But a Negro servant who had been stationed as warden at the door refused to allow the messenger to pass in, saying, 'The gemman can't be disturbed.'

"It seems that the messenger was aware of the contents of the note, or at least that it was a warning of the approach of the Americans, so, being foiled in his purpose of seeing Rall himself, he handed to note to the Negro with an order to carry it at once to Colonel Rall.

"The Negro obeyed, but Rall, excited with wine and interested in his game, merely thrust the note into his pocket and went on with his deal.

"Presently the roll of the American drums, the rattle of musketry, the tramp of horses, and the rumble of heavy gun carriages fell upon his drowsy ear, and in a moment he was wide awake, the cards were dropped, he sprang to his feet, and rushed away to his quarters and mounted his horse with all speed. But already by this time his soldiers were being driven by the Americans as chaff before the wind.

"The Hessians' drums were beating to arms, and a company rushed out of the barracks to protect the patrol. Washington's troops had begun to fight with an attack upon the outermost picket on the Pennington Road, and Stark, with the van of Sullivan's party, gave three cheers and rushed upon the enemy's picket near the river with their bayonets. They, astonished at the suddenness and fury of the charge, were seized with a panic and fled in confusion across the Assanpink.

"Both of the divisions—the one commanded by Washington, the other under Sullivan—now pressed forward so rapidly and with such zeal and determination that the Hessians were not allowed to form. Nor could they get possession of the two cannon in front of Rall's headquarters.

"The Americans themselves were forming in line of battle when Rall made his appearance, reeling in his saddle as if drunk—as I presume he was—received a report, then rode up in front of his regiment and called out, 'Forward, march; advance, advance!'

"But before his order could be obeyed a party of Americans hurried forward and dismounted his two cannon, accomplishing the feat without injury to themselves except that Captains William Washington and James Monroe were both slightly wounded."

"Where was General Washington then, mamma?"

"He was there in the midst of the fighting and exposed to the same dangers as his troops.

"It was under his personal direction that a battery of six guns was opened upon two regiments of Hessians less than three hundred yards distant. Washington was then near the front, a little to the right, where he could be easily seen by the enemy, and he made a target for their balls. But though his horse was wounded, he remained unhurt."

"Oh," cried Evelyn with enthusiasm, "surely God protected him and turned aside the balls, that America might not lose the one on whom so much depended — the father of his country, the ardent patriot, the best men and greatest of generals, as I do certainly believe he was!"

"I am proud that Washington was a countryman of mine!" exclaimed Rosie, her eyes sparkling.

"Yes, we are all proud of our Washington," said Lulu. "But what more can you tell us about the Battle of Trenton, Grandma Elsie?"

"Rall drew back his two regiments as if intending to reach the road to Princeton by turning Washington's left," continued Mrs. Travilla in reply. "To prevent that, an American regiment was thrown in front of him. It seemed likely that he might have forced a passage through it, but his troops, having collected much plunder in Trenton and wishing to hold on to it, persuaded him to try to recover the town.

"He made the attempt, but he was charged impetuously by the Americans and driven back further than before. In that movement he himself was mortally wounded by a musket ball. His men were thrown into confusion and presently surrendered.

"Then Baylor rode up to Washington and announced, 'Sir, the Hessians have surrendered.'"

"Baylor?" asked Walter. "Who was he, mamma?"

"One of Washington's aids," she replied. "In the first year of the war he was made an aide-de-camp to General Washington and in that capacity was with him in this battle."

"How I envy him!" exclaimed Lulu.

"I do think that if I'd been a man living in those days," said Walter, "I'd have cared for no greater honor than being an aide to our Washington."

His mother's only reply was a proudly affectionate look and smile as she went on with her story.

"And there was still another regiment, under Knyphausen, which had been ordered to cover the flank. These tried to reach the Assanpink Bridge, but they lost time in an effort to get two cannon out of the morass. When they reached the bridge, the Americans were guarding it on both sides. They tried to ford the river, but without success, and they presently surrendered to Lord Sterling—with the privilege of keeping their swords and their private baggage. That ended the battle, leaving the Americans with nearly a thousand prisoners on their hands.

"Over two hundred of the Hessians had escaped—some to Princeton, others to Bordentown. There were a hundred and thirty absent, having been sent out on some expedition, and seventeen were killed. The battle had lasted only thirty-five minutes, and the Americans had not lost a man."

"It was wonderful, I think!" said Evelyn in her earnest way. "Certainly God helped our patriotic forefathers or they never could have succeeded in their conflict with so powerful a foe as Great Britain was even then."

"It was all of God's great goodness to this land and people," said Grandma Elsie. "Had there been in that action defeat to our arms instead of victory, we would not—so soon at least—have become the free and powerful nation we are today. Congress lavished praise upon George Washington, but he replied, 'You pay me compliments as if the merit of the affair was due solely to me; but I assure you the other general officers who assisted me in the plan and execution have full as good a right to the encomium as myself.'"

"Possibly that was only just," remarked Rosie. "But it strikes me as very generous."

"It was just like Washington," said Walter. "Our Washington! I'm ever so proud of him!"

"As we all are," said his mother. "But we must not forget to give the glory of that victory and all others, and also of our final success, to Him who is the God of battles, and by whose strength and help our freedom was won. As Bancroft says, 'Until that hour the life of the United States flickered like a dying flame,' but God had appeared for their deliverance and from that time the hopes of the almost despairing people revived, while the confident expectations of their enemies were dashed to the ground. Lord George Germain exclaimed after he heard the news, 'All our hopes were blasted by the unhappy affair at Trenton.'"

"Unhappy affair indeed!" exclaimed Walter. "What a wicked, heartless wretch he must have been, mamma!"

"And how our poor soldiers did suffer!" sighed Lulu. "It makes my heart ache just to think of it!"

"And mine," said Grandma Elsie. "It is wonderful how much the poor fellows were willing to endure in the hope of attaining freedom for themselves and their country.

"Thomas Rodney tells us that on the night of the attack upon Trenton of which we have been talking, while Rall caroused and played cards beside his warm fire, our poor soldiers were toiling and suffering with cold and nakedness, facing wind and sleet in the defense of their country.

"'The night,'" he says, "'was as severe a night as ever I saw; the frost was sharp, the current difficult to stem, the ice increasing, the wind high, and at eleven it began to snow. It was three in the morning of the twenty-sixth before the troops and cannons were all over, and another hour passed before they could be formed on the Jersey side. A violent northeast storm of wind, sleet, and hail set in as they began their nine miles' march to Trenton, against an enemy in the best condition to fight. The weather was terrible for men clad as they were, and the ground slipped under their feet. For a mile and a half they had to climb a steep hill, from which they descended to the road that ran for about three miles between hills and forests of hickory, ash, and black oak.'"

"Oh, how brave and patriotic they were!" exclaimed Rosie. "I remember reading that their route might be easily traced by the blood on the snow from the feet of the poor fellows who had broken shoes or none. Oh, what a shame it was that Congress and the people let them — the men who were enduring so much and fighting so bravely for the liberty of both — bear such hardships!"

"It was, indeed," sighed Grandma Elsie. "It always gives me a heartache to think of those poor fellows marching through the darkness and that dreadful storm of snow, sleet, and bitter wind only half clothed. Just think of it! A continuous march of fifteen miles through darkness, over such a road, the storm directly in their faces. They reached their destination stiff with cold, yet rushed at once upon the foe, fighting bravely for freedom for themselves and their children. 'Victory or death,' was the watchword Washington had given them."

"Were they from all of the states, mamma?" asked Walter.

"They were principally Pennsylvania, Virginia, and New England troops," she answered. "Grant, the British commander in New Jersey, knew of the destitution of our troops but felt no fear that they would really venture to attack him—persuading himself that they would not cross the river because the floating ice would make it a difficult, if not impossible, thing for them to return.

"'Besides,' he wrote of it on the twenty-first, 'Washington's men have neither shoes nor stockings nor blankets, are almost naked, and dying of cold and want of food.'"

"And didn't Rall say the Americans wouldn't dare to come against him?" asked Walter.

"His reply to a warning of danger of being attacked was, 'Let them come; what need of entrenchments! We will come at them with the bayonet!'"

"But when they did come he was killed?"

"Yes, mortally wounded. He was taken by his aides and servants to his quarters at the house of a Quaker named Stacey Potts; and there Washington and Greene visited him just before leaving Trenton."

"They knew he was dying, mamma?"

"Yes, and, as Lossing tells us, Washington kindly offered such consolation as a soldier and Christian can bestow."

"It was very kind, and I hope Rall appreciated it."

"It would seem that he did, as the historian tells us it soothed the agonies of the expiring hero."

CHAPTER SEVENTH

FROM TRENTON, Grandma Elsie, the captain, and their young charges went on to Princeton, where they received a most joyful welcome from Harold and Herbert Travilla, now spending their last year at the seminary.

Their mother had written to them of the intended visit, and all necessary arrangements had been made. Carriages were in waiting, and shortly after their arrival, the whole party were on their way to the battleground, where the attention of the young people was drawn to the various points of interest, particularly the spot where General Mercer fell.

"The general's horse was wounded in the leg by a musket ball," explained Harold in reply to a question from his little brother. "He dismounted and was rallying his troops, when a British soldier felled him to the ground by a blow from a musket.

"He was supposed to be Washington. A shout was raised, 'The rebel general is taken!' and at that others of the enemy rushed to the spot calling out, 'Call for quarter, you d—d rebel!'"

"'I am no rebel!'" Mercer answered indignantly, though half a dozen of their bayonets were at his heart. And instead of calling for quarter, he continued to fight, striking at them with his sword till they bayoneted him and left him for dead.

"He was not dead, but he was mortally wounded.

"After the British had retreated he was carried to the house of Thomas Clark," continued Harold, pointing out the building as he spoke. "There he lingered in great pain till the twelfth and then died."

"I'm glad it wasn't Washington," said Walter.

"Was Washington hurt at all then, papa?" asked Gracie.

"No, though he was exposed to the hottest fire, he escaped without injury," replied the captain. "'Man is immortal till his work is done'—and Washington's was not done till years afterward."

"Not even when the war was over. He was our first president, I remember," said Lulu.

"Yes," replied her father. "And he did much for his country in that capacity.

"The night before this battle of Princeton he and his army were in a critical situation, the British being fully equal in numbers and their troops well disciplined, while about half of Washington's army was composed of raw militia—so that a general engagement the next day would be almost sure to result in defeat of the Americans.

"Washington called a council of war. It was himself who proposed to withdraw from their present position—on the high ground upon the southern bank of the Assanpink—before dawn of the next morning, and, by a circuitous march to Princeton, get in the rear of the enemy, attack them at that place, and if successful march on to New Brunswick and take or destroy their stores there.

"The great difficulty in the way was that the ground was too soft from a thaw to make it safe and easy to move their forty pieces of cannon.

"But a kind Providence removed that hindrance, the weather suddenly becoming so extremely cold that in two hours or less the roads were hard enough for the work."

"As Lossing says," remarked Grandma Elsie, "'The great difficulty was overcome by a power mightier than that of man. Our fathers were fighting for God-given rights and it was by His help they at last succeeded.'"

"What's the rest of the story?" asked Walter. "How did Washington and his army slip away without the British seeing them? For I suppose they had sentinels awake and out."

"Washington had a number of camp fires lighted along his front," replied Harold, to whom the question seemed to be addressed. "They made the fires of the fences near at hand. That made the British think he was encamped for the night, and Cornwallis, when someone urged him to make an attack that night, said he would certainly 'catch the fox in the morning.' The fox, of course, was Washington, but he didn't catch him. It was not till dawn he discovered that the fox had eluded him and slipped away, fleeing so silently that the British did not know in what direction he had gone till they heard the boom of cannon in the fight here.

"Cornwallis thought it was thunder, but Sir William Erskine recognized it as what it was and exclaimed, 'To arms, General! Washington has out-generaled us. Let us fly to the rescue at Princeton.'"

"How long did the battle last?" queried Walter.

"The fight right here lasted about fifteen minutes, but it was very severe," replied his brother. "Then Washington pushed on to Princeton, and in a ravine near the college, they had another sharp fight with the Fifty-fifth British Regiment."

"And whipped them, too?"

"Yes. They were soon flying toward Brunswick with the Fortieth Regiment going along with them.

"A part of a regiment was still in the college buildings, and Washington had some cannon placed in proper position, then began firing on them. One of the balls—it is said to have been the first—passed into the chapel and through the portrait of George the Second that hung in a large frame on the wall. A few more shots were fired, and then the Princeton militia and some other daring fellows, burst open a door of Nassau Hall and called upon the troops there to surrender, which they promptly did."

"And Cornwallis had not reached there, yet?" Walter inquired.

"No," returned Harold. "And when he did arrive he found that the battle was over, and Washington, with his victorious troops and prisoners, had already left the town and was in hot pursuit of the fleeing Fortieth and Fifty-fifth Regiments."

"Our poor fellows so tired and cold!" sighed Eva.

"Yes," said the captain. "They fought at Trenton on the twenty-sixth, after being up, probably, all night getting across the river, had spent the next night in marching upon Princeton and the next day in fighting. So that they must have been terribly fatigued even had they had the warm clothing and nourishing food they needed, but less than half of them had been able to procure any breakfast or dinner. And as you all know, many of them were without shoes or stockings. Ah, how we should prize the liberty which was so dearly bought!"

"So to save his army," resumed Harold, "Washington refrained from an effort to seize the rich prize at New Brunswick and let them rest that night and refresh themselves with food. He then retired to his winter quarters at Morristown.

"Now, good people, if you are ready to retrace your steps, let us go back and look at the town souvenirs of the Revolution — among them the portrait of Washington in the frame that used to hold that of George the Second."

Family and friends made but a short stay at Princeton, leaving that evening, and the next day they visited the scene of the Battle of Monmouth. The captain gave a rapid sketch of the movements of the opposing armies, as he did so pointing out the various positions of the different corps, describing Lee's disgraceful conduct at the beginning of the fight, telling of the just indignation of Washington, his stern reproof, Lee's angry rejoinder, and then with what consummate skill and dispatch his errors were repaired by the general-in-chief. He told how the retreating, almost routed, troops rallied, how order was brought out of confusion, and how fearlessly he exposed himself to the iron storm while giving his orders so that that patriot army, which had been so near destruction, within half an hour was drawn up in battle array and ready to meet the foe.

"It was a very hot day that day, wasn't it, papa?" asked Lulu.

"One of the hottest of the season," replied her father. "Ninety-six degrees in the shade, and the sun slew his victims on both sides."

"Don't you think Lee was a traitor, captain?" queried Evelyn.

"Either that or insane. I think it would have been a happy thing for America if both he and Gaines had remained in their own land. They did the

American cause far more harm than good. Though I by no means accuse Gaines of treachery, he was envious of Washington, and he was so desirous to supersede him that he was ready to sacrifice the cause to that end."

"I just wish he'd been sent back to England," said Walter. "But please tell us the rest about the battle, brother Levis, won't you?"

The captain willingly complied.

"It was a dreadful battle," remarked Evelyn with a sigh, as his story came to a conclusion.

"Yes, one of the most hotly contested of the war," he assented. "It resulted in victory to the Americans in spite of Lee's repeated assertion that the 'attempt was madness.'

"All the other American generals did well, the country resounded with praises for Washington, and Congress passed a unanimous vote of thanks to him 'for his great and good conduct and victory.'"

"It was in this battle Captain Molly fought, wasn't it?" asked Rosie.

"Yes," the captain replied. Noticing the eagerly inquiring looks of Gracie and Walter, he went on to tell the story. Molly was the wife of the cannoneer who was firing one of the field pieces, while she, disregarding the danger from the shots of the enemy, made frequent journeys to and from a spring near at hand, thus furnishing her husband with the means of slacking his thirst, which must have been great at his work in such weather.

"At length a shot from the enemy killed him, and an order was given to remove the cannon, as there was no one among the soldiers near who was capable of its management.

"But Molly, who had seen her husband fall and heard the order, dropped her bucket, sprang to the cannon, seized the rammer, and vowing that she would avenge his death, fired it with surprising skill, performing the duty probably as well as if she had belonged to the sterner sex.

"The next morning General Greene presented her—just as she was, all covered with dust and blood—to Washington, who gave her the commission of sergeant as a reward for her bravery. In addition to that he recommended her to Congress as worthy to have her name placed upon the list of those enlisted to half-pay during life.

"The French officers so admired her bravery that they made her many presents. Lossing tells us that she would sometimes pass along the lines and get her cocked hat full of crowns. He also says the widow of General Hamilton told him she had often seen 'Captain Molly,' as she was called, and described her as red-haired, freckled-faced, young Irish woman with a handsome, piercing eye."

"Papa, did Captain Molly really wear a man's hat?" asked Gracie.

"Yes, and also an artilleryman's coat over her woman's petticoats. She had done a brave deed about nine months before the Battle of Monmouth, when Fort Clinton was taken by the British. She was there with her husband when the fort was attacked, and when the Americans retreated from the fort and the enemy was scaling the ramparts, her husband dropped his match and fled, but Molly picked it up and fired the gun, then scampered off after him. That was the last gun fired in the fort by the Americans."

"This battle of Monmouth was a great victory for us — for the Americans, I mean?" Walter asked.

"Yes, in spite of the shameful retreat of Lee and the unaccountable detention of Morgan and his brave riflemen, who were within sound of the fearful tumult of the battle and eager to take part in it. Morgan was striding to and fro in an agony of suspense, and desirous to participate in the struggle, yet unaccountably detained where he was."

"And that was some of that traitor Lee's doings, I suspect," exclaimed Lulu hotly. "Wasn't it, papa?"

"My child, I do not know," returned the captain. "But it seems altogether probable that if Morgan could have fallen with his fresh troops upon the weary ones of Sir Henry Clinton toward the close of the day, the result might have been such a surrender as Burgoyne was forced to make at Saratoga.

"But as it was, while Washington and his weary troops slept that night, the general looking forward to certain victory in the morning, when he could again attack his country's foes with his own troops strengthened and refreshed by sleep, Sir Henry and his troops stole silently away and hurried toward Sandy Hook."

"Did Washington chase him?" asked Walter.

"No," said the captain. "When he considered the start the British had, the weariness of his own troops, the excessive heat of the weather, and the deep, sandy country, with but little water to be had, he thought it wiser not to make the attempt."

"Papa, was it near here that the British shot Mrs. Caldwell?" asked Lulu.

"No, Lulu, that occurred in a place called Connecticut Farms, about four miles northwest of

Elizabethtown, to which they — the Caldwells — had removed for greater safety.

"It was in June of 1780. The British under Clinton and Knyphausen crossed over to Elizabethtown and moved on toward Springfield. The Americans, under General Greene, were posted upon the Short Hills, a series of high ridges near Springfield, and came down to the plain to oppose the invasion of the British. I will not go into the details of the battle, but merely say that the British were finally repulsed, Greene being so advantageously posted by that time that he was anxious for an engagement, but Knyphausen, perceiving his own disadvantage, retreated, setting fire to the village of Connecticut Farms — now called Union — on his way.

"The people of the town immediately fled when they perceived the approach of the British, but Mrs. Caldwell remained, and with her children and maid, she retired to a private apartment and engaged in prayer.

"Presently her maid, glancing from a window, exclaimed that a red-coated soldier had jumped over the fence and was coming toward the window.

"At that Mrs. Caldwell rose from the bed where she had been sitting, and at that moment the soldier raised his musket and deliberately fired at her through the window, sending two balls through her body, killing her instantly, so that she fell dead among her poor, frightened children.

"It was with some difficulty that her body was saved from the fire that was consuming the town. It was dragged out into the street and lay there for some time — several hours — till some friends got leave to remove it to a house.

"Her husband was at the Short Hills that night, and he was in great anxiety and distress about his family. The next day he went with a flag of truce to the village, found it in ruins, and his wife dead.

"That cold-blooded act of murder and wanton destruction of the peaceful little village aroused great indignation all over the land and turned many a Tory into a Whig."

"Did anybody ever find out who it was that killed her, papa?" asked Gracie.

"The murderer is said to have been a man from the north of Ireland, named McDonald, who for some unknown reason had taken a violent dislike to Mr. Caldwell.

"A little more than a year afterward Mr. Caldwell himself was slain in a very similar fashion, but by an American soldier."

"An American, brother Levis?" exclaimed Walter, in unfeigned surprise. "Did he do it intentionally?"

"The shooting was intentional, but whether meant to kill I cannot say," replied the captain. "The fellow who did it is said to have been a drunken Irishman. It happened at Elizabethtown, then in possession of the Americans. A sloop made weekly trips between that place and New York, where the headquarters of the British army were at that time and frequently carried passengers with a flag and also parcels.

"The Americans had a very strong guard at a tavern near the shore, and one or two sentinels paced the causeway that extended across the marsh to the wharf.

"One day in November of 1781, the vessel came with a lady on board who had permission to visit her sister at Elizabethtown, and Mr. Caldwell drove down to the wharf in his chaise to receive her. Then, not finding her on the wharf, he went aboard the sloop and presently returned, carrying a small bundle.

"The sentinel on the causeway halted Mr. Caldwell and demanded the bundle for examination, saying he had been ordered not to let anything of the kind pass without strict investigation.

"Mr. Caldwell refused to give it to the man— James Morgan, by name—saying it was the property of a lady and had been merely put in his care.

"The sentinel repeated his demand, and Mr. Caldwell turned and went back toward the vessel— it is presumed to carry the bundle back to its owner, when the sentinel leveled his piece and shot him dead upon the spot.

"Morgan was arrested, tried for murder, and hung. He was first taken to the church, where a sermon was preached from the text 'Oh, do not this abominable thing which I hate.'

"Mr. Caldwell had been much beloved as a pious and excellent minister. He was shot on Saturday afternoon, and the next day many people came in to attend church knowing nothing of the dreadful deed that had been done till they arrived.

"Then there was a great sound of weeping and lamentation. The corpse was placed on a large stone at the door of the house of a friend whither it had been carried, and all who wished to do so were allowed to take a last look at the remains of their beloved pastor. Then, before the coffin was closed, Dr. Elias Boudinot led the nine orphaned children up to the coffin to take their last look at the face of their father, and, as they stood weeping there, made a most moving address in their behalf."

꙳ ꙳ ꙳ ꙳ ꙳

A few more days were spent by the party in and about Philadelphia, during which brief visits were paid to places interesting to them because of the Revolution — Whitemarsh, Germantown, Barren Hill, Valley Forge, as well as those within the city itself.

But the summer heats were over, and the hearts of one and all began to yearn for the sweets of home — all the more when word reached them through the mails that the members of their party left in the Newport cottages had already succumbed to the same sort of sickness and were on their homeward way by land. A day or two later the *Dolphin*, with her full complement of passengers, was moving rapidly southward.

CHAPTER EIGHTH

MAX HAD A MOST pleasant surprise when the mail was distributed on that first morning after his arrival at the Naval Academy. Till his name was called, he had hardly hoped there would be anything for him. But then as a letter was handed him, and he recognized upon it his father's well-known writing, his cheek flushed and his eyes shone.

A hasty glance at his mates showed him that each seemed intent upon his own affairs—no one watching him—so he broke the seal and read with swelling heart the few sentences of fatherly advice and affection the captain had found time to pen before the *Dolphin* weighed anchor the previous evening. He knew the homesickness that would assail his son on that first day of separation from himself and all composing the dear home circle, and he was fain to relieve it so far as lay in his power.

Max read the letter twice, then, refolding it, slipped it in into his pocket to read again and ponder upon when he could find a moment of leisure and freedom from observation.

More firmly convinced than ever, if that were possible, was the lad that his was the best, kindest, and dearest of fathers.

"And if I don't do him credit and make him happy and proud of his first-born, it shall not be for want of trying," was his mental resolve.

It was fortunate for Max that his father had been seen and admired by the cadets, who one and all thought him a splendid specimen of naval officer and were, therefore, well disposed toward his son.

But Max himself had such a bright, intelligent face and genial manner, was so ready to assist or oblige a comrade in any right and honorable way that lay in his power, so very conscientious about obeying rules and doing his duty in everything, and brave in facing ridicule, insolence, and contempt when the choice was between that and wrong-doing, that no one of them could help respecting him, whether willing to acknowledge it or not.

At first the "plebes," or boys in the same class, who had entered in June of the same year, showed a disposition to treat him, as well as the other "Seps," as the lads entering in September are styled, with scorn, as knowing less than themselves. But that soon changed under the exhibition Max was able to make of all he had learned from his father during the weeks on board the *Dolphin*, showing himself perfectly at home in "rigging-loft work," rowing, and swimming, and he was by no means slow in taking to great-gun exercise, infantry tactics, and field artillery.

Nor was he less ready in the art of swinging a hammock. His father had not neglected that part of his education, and Hunt and others who had hoped for some fun in watching his maiden effort had to own themselves defeated and disappointed. Max was an expert at that as the oldest member of the class.

So the "plebes" presently dropped their air of conscious superiority and soon began to treat him as an equal—a change which he reported to his father with evident satisfaction. He wrote frequently and with much openness to that father, telling of his duties and pleasures and asking advice in any perplexity as freely as he could have asked it of anyone near his own age and with full confidence in the wisdom and the affection for him which would dictate the reply.

Nor was he disappointed. Almost every single day a letter came from the captain, breathing strong fatherly affection; giving commendation, encouragement, and the best of advice; and telling everything about the doings and happenings in the family that was not related by Mamma Vi or one of Max's sisters, who not infrequently added a note to papa's larger letter.

All those letters, like the first, were highly prized by the recipient and read and reread in leisure moments till he could have repeated their contents almost word for word. Every perusal increased the lad's desire and determination to be and do all those dear ones—especially his father—could wish. and also to please and honor Him to whose service he had consecrated his life and all his powers.

Max was not perfect, but he was honest and true and sincerely desirous to do right.

He was much interested in the accounts received of the visits of his father and the others to the scenes of Revolutionary events in Pennsylvania and New Jersey, and, though far from regretting his choice of a profession, could not help wishing he could have made one of the touring party.

One day, after he had spent some weeks in the Academy, he was disappointed in his expectation of receiving a letter. None came the next day either, but then it occurred to him that the *Dolphin* was probably on her homeward way, and he would soon get a letter from Woodburn, telling of the arrival there of all belonging to the dear home circle.

And he was right. A package of letters came presently giving an account of the events of the last days spent in Philadelphia, the return voyage, and the joy of the arrival at their own beautiful and happy home.

As Max read, how he longed to be with them! Yet the concluding sentences of his father's letter restored him to contentment with things as they were.

The captain had just received and read the report of his boy's conduct and academic standing for the first month and was much pleased with it. He made that very clear to the lad, calling him his dear son, his joy and pride, and telling him that until he was a father himself he would never know the joy and happiness such a report of a son's behavior and improvement of his opportunities could give.

"Ah," thought the boy, "I'll try harder than ever since it gives such pleasure to my kindest and best of fathers. How glad I am to have the chance! How thankful I ought to be! I doubt if there was ever a more fortunate boy than myself."

Max and his roommate, Hunt, liked each other from the first, and seldom had even the slightest of disagreements.

According to the rules they took turns, week about, in keeping their room in order, each trying to outdo his mate in the thoroughness with which he attended to all the minutia of the business.

They were good-natured rivals in other matters connected with the course of instruction they were going through: gymnastic exercises, fencing and boxing, and the drill called fire-quarters, in which the whole battalion was formed into a fire-brigade. When the fire-bell is sounded each cadet hastened to his proper place in the troop, and the steam engine and hose-carriages belonging to the Academy were brought out and used as they would be in case some building were in flames and the cadets were called upon to assist in extinguishing the blaze.

Max and his chum had become quite expert at that exercise, when one night they were roused from sleep by the sound of the fire-bell. Springing up and running to their window, they saw that a dwelling several squares from the Academy was in flames.

"It's a real fire this time!" cried Hunt, snatching up a garment and beginning a very hurried dressing, Max doing the same. "Now we'll have a chance to show how well we understand the business of putting it out."

An hour or more of great excitement and exertion followed, then, the fire extinguished, the brigade returned to the Academy and the lads to their sleeping-room, so weary with their exertions that they were very soon sound asleep again.

The experience of that night furnished Max with material for an interesting letter to his father and the rest of the home folks.

"I didn't know the cadets were taught how to put out fires," remarked Gracie, when her father had finished reading aloud Max's story of the doings of the cadets on that night to his wife and children.

"Yes, that is an important part of their education. There are many things a cadet needs to know."

"I suppose so, papa," said Lulu. "Though Maxie doesn't say much about his own share in the work, I feel very sure he did his part. And aren't you proud of him—your eldest son?"

"I am afraid I am," replied her father with a smile in his eyes. "It may be all parental partiality, but my boy seems to be one of whom any father might well be proud."

"And I am quite of your opinion, my dear," said Violet. "I am very proud of my husband's son—the dear, good, brave fellow."

But the captain's eyes were again upon the letter, his face expressing both interest and amusement.

"What is it, Levis?" she asked. "Something more that you can share with the rest of us?"

"Yes," he returned, then read aloud.

"'That was Friday night, and this is Saturday evening. This afternoon Hunt and I were allowed to go into the city. We were walking along one of the side streets and came upon a man who was beating his horse most unmercifully.

"'The poor thing was just a bag of bones that seemed to have nothing but skin over them, and he was hitched to a cart heavily loaded with earth and stones. Its head was down, and it looked ready to drop, while the savage wretch—not worthy to be called a man—was beating it furiously and cursing and swearing in a towering passion. Men and boys gathered around, some calling him to stop.

"'But he didn't pay the smallest attention, till the poor beast spoke—at least the voice seemed to come from its mouth—"Aren't you ashamed to be beating me so, and swearing at me, too, when you've starved me till I haven't strength to drag even myself another step?"

"'At that the man stopped both his beating and swearing, and he stood looking scared out of his wits. The crowd, too, looked thunderstruck, and presently one fellow said, "It's the story of Balaam and his donkey over again. There must be an angel somewhere round," glancing from side to side as he spoke in a way that almost made me laugh, angry as I was at the human brute, or rather the inhuman scoundrel, who had been treating the poor creature so cruelly.

"'Others looked, too, but they didn't seem to be able to see the angel.

"'Hunt, standing close at my side, gave a low whistle. "What, upon earth?" he said. "Oh, there must be a ventriloquist somewhere in the crowd. I'd like to know who he is. Wouldn't you, Max?"

"'"Do you really think that's the explanation?" I asked. "Certainly," he answered in a tone as if he was rather disgusted at my stupidity. "How else could you account for the seeming ability of that wretched animal to talk?"

"'"I can't think of any other explanation," I answered. "But I hope that inhuman wretch of a driver doesn't know anything about ventriloquists and so will be afraid to ill-use the poor creature any more." "I hope so, indeed," Hunt said. "See, the people are stroking and patting it, and yonder comes a man with a bucket of water and another with a panful of oats. The ventriloquist has done some good."

"'"I'm glad of it," I replied. Then, looking at my watch, I saw that it was high time for us to go back to the Academy.

"'Hunt told the story to some of the other fellows that evening, and there was great wonderment about the ventriloquist. A good many wished they could have a chance to see him and some of his tricks. Some of them remarked in a wondering way that I seemed very indifferent about it, and then I told them of Cousin Ronald and his doings at Ion, which interested them very much. Several said they would like greatly to make his acquaintance and see and hear what he could do. Isn't it good, papa, that they have never once suspected me?'"

"Well!" exclaimed Lulu. "Max used his talent to do good that time. Didn't he, papa?"

"He did, indeed," replied the captain. "I hope that poor horse will, as a consequence, receive better treatment in the future."

"I'm so glad Maxie could frighten the man so and make him stop treating it so dreadfully," remarked Gracie with a sigh of relief. "I never thought before that that talent of his would be good for anything but to make fun for folks."

"The ability to afford amusement to others is a talent not to be despised," said her father. "Innocent mirth often does good like a medicine, but power to rescue even a beast from ill-treatment is still more to be coveted, and I shall be glad indeed if Max will use his gifts in that way whenever opportunity offers."

CHAPTER NINTH

A WEEK OR MORE had passed since the return of the party from their vacation in the more northern part of their loved native land, and Lulu and Gracie, who had at first missed their older brother sorely from the family circle, had now begun to feel somewhat accustomed to his absence and were very merry and happy.

They had resumed their studies, reciting, as before, to their father. They took daily walks and rides on their ponies, varied by an occasional drive with the captain, Violet, and the little ones.

The Ion and Fairview families, too, had gone back to old pleasures and employments. But so busy had all been, taking up familiar cares and duties and making needed preparations for the approaching winter, that only few and short visits had as yet been exchanged between them.

The Woodburn family had been in the sitting room, just after breakfast, when the captain had read Max's letter aloud to his wife and children.

"Go to the schoolroom now, daughters, and look over your lessons for the day," he said presently, addressing Lulu and Gracie.

They obeyed instantly, and as they left the room a servant came in with a note from Violet's mother, which he handed to his mistress, saying one of the Ion servants had just brought it.

"Mamma's handwriting," Violet remarked to her husband, as she took the note and glanced at the address upon it.

"Ah! I hope they are all well?" he inquired.

"No, mamma herself is certainly not quite well," Violet answered with a disturbed look, after glancing hastily down the page. "She says as much, and that she wants me to come and spend a few days with her, bringing all the children if I choose — they will not disturb her. And you also will be most welcome. Dear, dear mamma! I shall go to her at once — unless my husband objects," she added, looking up at him with a rather sad sort of smile.

"As he certainly could not think of doing, my love," he replied, in tender tones. "We must go, of course — you and the little ones, at least. We will consider about the older ones, and I shall spend my time between the two places, not being willing to stay constantly away from you, yet having some matters to attend to here and some things that ought not to be delayed."

"But you will be with us a part of every day?" returned Violet with a wistful look up into his face.

"Yes, oh, yes!" he hastened to say. "With my wife so near at hand I could not let a day go by without inflicting my presence upon her for some small part of it," he concluded in a half-jesting tone and with a fond look down into the sweet, troubled face.

"I think it could not be harder for you than for me, my dear," she returned with a loving smile up at him. "I should like to take all the children," she went on. "But Alma is here to make some dresses for Lulu, and she will need her at hand to try them on and make sure of the fit."

"And I should seriously object to allowing Lulu to drop her studies again just as she has made a fresh start with them," said the captain. "So I think she will have to stay at home. Gracie also, I think, as there would be the same objection to her absence from home, as regards the lessons I mean."

"But if you will allow it, I can hear her recite at Ion," said Violet. "She could learn her lessons there and still have a good deal of time to play with her little sister, who thinks no one else quite equal to her Gracie for a playfellow."

"Well, my dear, we will make that arrangement if you wish it," responded the captain.

"And yet how Lulu will miss her," Violet said, a troubled look coming over face. "I wish we could manage it so that she could go, too, the dear child!"

"I should be glad to give her the pleasure," returned Captain Raymond. "But really I think it will not do to have her studies so interfered with now when she has but just settled down to them. It will be a little hard for her but perhaps not a bad lesson in patience and self-denial."

"But a lesson I fear she will not enjoy," remarked Violet with a regretful smile.

Going into the schoolroom presently, the captain found his two little girls industriously busy with their tasks.

"Gracie, daughter," he said, "your mamma is going over to Ion for a few days, because Grandma Elsie is not very well and wants her companionship. Mamma Vi wants you — for little Elsie's sake, having found you very successful in entertaining her and baby Ned — to accompany her. We are all invited, of course, but I must be here the greater part of the time, as I have various matters to oversee. Lulu cannot be spared from home as Alma is at work upon some dresses for her, and I wish her to go on diligently with her studies."

"But don't I need to be attending to mine, papa?" queried Gracie, looking regretfully at her sister, over whose face had come a look of keen disappointment succeeding one of pleased anticipation called out by the beginning of her father's present communication.

"Yes," he said with a smile. "We are going to let you attend to them there with Mamma Vi acting as your governess."

"Isn't she willing to do the same for me, too, papa?" asked Lulu in a slightly hurt tone.

"I think so," he answered pleasantly. "But there is the dressmaking, and I couldn't think of such a thing as asking to have that carried to Ion."

Lulu seemed to have nothing more to say and Gracie gave her a troubled look. Then, with a little hesitation, "Papa," she said, "I—I think I'd rather stay at home with Lu, if I may."

"No, daughter," he answered, still speaking very pleasantly. "I have not time to give my reasons just now, but I want you to go and Lulu to stay. It will probably be for only a few days, and I think she may trust her father not to allow her to be very lonely in the meanwhile," he added with a smile directed at Lulu. But she did not seem to see it, keeping her face down and her eyes fixed upon her book.

He then left the room, saying to Gracie as he went out, "Make haste, daughter, to gather up your books and whatever else you may wish to take with you. I have already ordered the carriage and there is no time to waste. Lulu may help you if she will."

"Will you help me, Lu?" asked Gracie with a very sympathizing look at her sister. "Oh, I wish papa had said you were to go, too! Whatever shall I do without my dear, big sister!"

"Never mind, Gracie. I'm sure I don't want to go where I'm not wanted," replied Lulu in a hurt tone.

"I'm sure it isn't because they wouldn't like to have you there," returned Gracie, running to her sister and putting her arms about her neck.

"Why don't they ask me, then?" queried Lulu a little angrily.

"Maybe they did. I'm 'most sure Grandma Elsie wouldn't forget to include you in her invitation. Oh, yes, don't you remember papa did say we were all invited? But you know there are the lessons, and I suppose papa would rather hear them himself."

"But he could hear them there."

"Yes, so he could if he wanted to. But then there's the dressmaking, you know."

"That could be put off a few days," returned Lulu with a very grownup air. "There are plenty of ways when people want to do a thing—plenty of excuses to be thought of when they don't. Alma has numerous customers and could sew for somebody else first, giving her my time and me hers after we get home."

"Oh, maybe it could be managed in that way!" exclaimed Gracie joyously. "And I'd so much rather have you along. I think I'll ask papa."

"No, don't you do any such thing," returned Lulu. "If I'm not wanted, I'm sure I don't wish to go. But you'll have to hurry, Gracie. You know papa is very particular about our being prompt in obeying his orders."

"Yes," returned Gracie, who was again at her desk. "But I have been busy all this time getting out the books and other things I must take alone, and now I'll go upstairs and get dressed and put up the things there that I want. Won't you go with me? You'll know so much better than I what I need to take."

"Yes, Gracie, dear. I'll be glad to give you all the help I can. I'm glad papa said I might. Oh, but it will be lonely here without you! I do think papa might have said I could go, too."

"I'd be ever so glad if he had, or would," said Gracie, as hand in hand they left the room together. "But you know, Lu, dear, we always find out in the end that his way is the best."

"So we do, and I'll try to believe it now," returned Lulu in a more cheerful tone than she had used since learning that the rest of the family were to go on to Ion and she was to remain at home.

With Lulu's good help Gracie was ready in a few minutes, and just then they heard their father call to her to come at once, as the carriage was at the door.

The sisters embraced each other hastily, Gracie saying, "Oh, Lu, good-bye. I do wish you were going along, too, for I can hardly bear to go along without you."

"Never mind, but just try to enjoy yourself as much as ever you can," returned Lulu. "Go down now, dearie, for we should never keep papa waiting, you know. Here's Agnes to carry down your satchel. I hope you won't stay long enough away from me to need many clothes. If you do it will be easy enough to send them — the carriage going back and forth every day."

Gracie was halfway down the stairs before Lulu had finished.

"Ain't you gwine down to see de folks off, Miss Lulu?" queried Agnes, as she took up the satchel.

"No," returned Lulu shortly. "I'm going back to the schoolroom to attend to my lessons."

Agnes gave her a look of surprise as she left the room, thinking she had never known Miss Lu to fail to be at the door when any of the other members of the family were leaving for more than a short drive, and she staying behind.

"Where is Lulu, Gracie?" asked Violet, as the captain handed the little girl into the carriage. "I hadn't time to hunt her up, and I thought she would be here at the door to say good-bye to us all."

"She said she must hurry back to her lessons, mamma," answered Gracie, blushing for her sister. "You see she stopped to help me get ready, and I suppose she's afraid she'll not know them well by the time papa wants to hear her recite."

"It would have taken very little of her time," the captain remarked with a grave and somewhat displeased look.

"Oh, well, you can bring her over to Ion, perhaps this afternoon or tomorrow for a call, Levis," Violet hastened to say in a cheery tone.

"Possibly," he answered, and he was about to step into the carriage when a servant came hurrying up to ask directions in regard to some work to be done on the grounds.

"My dear," said the captain to Violet, "I think it would be better for you and the children to drive on without waiting for me. I shall probably follow you in another hour or two."

"Very well, my darling. Please don't disappoint us if you can help it," returned Violet, and the carriage drove on, while Captain Raymond walked away in the opposite direction to give the needed orders to his men.

✄ ✄ ✄ ✄ ✄

"I think it's a shame that I should be left behind when all the rest of the family are going to Ion to have a good time," muttered Lulu angrily, as she seated herself at her desk again and opened a book. "Papa could hear my lessons there just as well as here if he chose, and Mamma Vi might have arranged to have my dresses made a week or two later."

"Miss Lu," said Agnes, opening the door and putting in her head, "Miss Alma tole me for to tell you she's 'bout ready fo' to try on yo' new dress."

"Tell her to take it to my room. I'll go up there to have it tried on," replied Lulu in a vexed tone.

Then, as Agnes withdrew her head and closed the door, she cried, "Horrid thing! Why couldn't she have come to me while I was up there? Here I am, hardly fairly settled to my work, and I must drop it and go back again. I'd better take my book with me while she alters something that she has got wrong, for she's generally too stupid to make a thing right at the first trial. Well, perhaps she'll get done by the time papa comes back and is ready to hear me recite."

So saying, she went slowly from the schoolroom and upstairs to her own apartment.

There were a few minutes of waiting for Alma, which did not improve Lulu's temper. As the girl came in, she received an angry glance, accompanied by the remark in no very pleasant tones that she had no business to send for people till she was ready to attend to them.

At that Alma colored painfully. "I am sorry to have inconvenienced you, Miss Lu," she said. "I'll try not to keep you so very long."

"If you don't, it will be about the first time that you haven't," snapped Lulu. "I think you are just about the slowest, most blundering dressmaker I ever did see."

At that unkind remark, Alma's eyes filled with tears, but she went on silently with her work, making no rejoinder. Lulu—the reproaches of her own conscience rendering her uneasy and irritable—fidgeted and fussed, thus greatly increasing the difficulty of the task.

"Miss Lu," Alma said at last in a despairing tone, "if you can't keep more still, it is not possible for me to make the dress fit you right."

"Indeed!" returned Lulu scornfully. "I don't feel sure of your ability to fit it right under any circumstances—such a stupid, awkward thing as you are, and—"

Her sentence left unfinished, for at that instant, to her astonishment and dismay, her father's voice called to her from his dressing room in sterner accents than she had heard from him in a long while. "Lucilla, come here to me!" She had not known of his detention at home, but had supposed he had gone with the others to Ion.

Jerking off the waist, which Alma had already unfastened, snatching up a dressing sack, and putting it on as she went, she appeared before him blushing and shamefaced.

"I am both surprised and mortified by what I have just overheard," he said. "I had a better opinion of my eldest daughter than to suppose she would ever show herself so heartless. You surely must have forgotten that poor Alma is in a strange land, while you are at home in your father's house. Go to her now and apologize for your rudeness."

Lulu made no movement to obey, but she stood before him in sullen silence and with downcast, scowling countenance.

He waited a moment then said sternly, "Lucilla, you will yield instant obedience to my order or go immediately to your own room and not venture into my presence again until you can tell me that you have obeyed."

At that she turned and left the room, more angry and rebellious than she had ever been since that dreadful time at Ion when her indulgence in a fit of passion had so nearly cost little Elsie's life.

"Papa will have a pretty time making me do it," she muttered angrily to herself as she stood by a window in her bedroom looking out into the grounds. "Ask Alma's pardon, indeed! She's not even a lady. She's nothing but a poor woman, who has to support herself with her needle—or rather with a sewing machine, cutting and fitting—and I think it's just outrageous for papa to tell me I must ask her pardon. I'll not do it, and papa needn't think he can make me. Though—" she added, uneasily, the next minute, "to be sure, he always has made me obey him. But I'm older now—too old, I think, even he would say, to be whipped into doing what I don't choose to do.

"But he forbade me to come into his presence till I obeyed, and—oh, dear, I can't live that way, because I love him so. I love him better than anyone else in all the wide world, and—and—it would just kill me to have to go without his love and his caresses—never to have him hug and kiss me and call me his dear child, his darling. Oh, I couldn't bear it! I never could! It would just break my heart!" And her tears began to fall like rain.

She cried quite violently for a while, and then she began to think of Alma more kindly and pityingly than ever before, as an orphan and a stranger in a strange land.

"Oh, I am ashamed to have treated her so!" she exclaimed at length. "I will ask her pardon—not only because papa has ordered me to do so, but because I am sorry for her and really mortified to think of having treated her so badly."

Fortunately, just at that moment Alma's timid rap was heard at the door and her voice saying in a hesitating way, "Miss Lu, please, I need to try the dress once more. I'm very sorry to disturb and trouble you, but I know you want it to be a good fit."

"Yes, of course I do, Alma," returned Lulu gently, opening the door as she spoke. "You are quite right to come back with it. I'm sorry and ashamed of having been so rude and unkind to you when you were in here before," she added, holding out her hand. "It was shameful treatment. Papa said I must ask your pardon, and I think I would do it now, even if he hadn't ordered me."

"It is too much, Miss Lu," Alma said, blushing, and with tears in her eyes. "I could never ask such a thing as that of a young lady like you."

"My behavior has been unladylike today," sighed Lulu. "And papa is very, very displeased with me."

"I am sorry," Alma responded in a sympathizing tone. "But the captain will not stay angry. He is so very fond of his children."

"Yes, and he is so kind and indulgent that I ought to be the best girl in the world. Oh, I wish I had not behaved so badly!"

"He will forgive you, Miss. He will not stay displeased, for his love for you is so very great," returned Alma. "There, Miss, the dress does fit you now. See in the glass. Does it not?"

"Yes," Lulu replied, surveying herself in the mirror. "I could not ask a better fit, Alma."

"It is lovely, Miss Lu. The material is so fine and soft, and the colors are so beautiful!" remarked the girl, gazing upon it with admiring eyes. "It is good, Miss Lu, to have a kind papa, rich enough to gif you all things needful for a young lady to wear."

"Yes, and so generous and kind as mine is," sighed Lulu. "It is a very, very great shame that I ever do anything to displease him."

Alma went back to the sewing room, and Lulu hastened to the door of the room where her father had been when he called her. But a glance within showed her that he was not there now. Then she ran downstairs and through the library, parlors, halls—everywhere—looking for him.

"Oh, where is he?" she sighed. "I must find him and tell him how sorry I am for my naughtiness. I can't have one minute of happiness till I have done so and received my kiss of forgiveness."

Snatching a hat from the rack and putting it on as she went, she ran out and around the porches and the grounds, but he was nowhere to be seen.

"Miss Lu," called a servant at length, "is you lookin' fo' de cap'n? He's done gone to Ion, I 'spects, kase dere's whar Miss Wi'let went in de kerridge."

"Did he say when he would come back?" asked Lulu, steadying her voice with quite an effort.

"He gwine come back dis evenin' fo' suah, Miss Lu, to see 'bout de work on de plantation," was the reply, as the man turned to his employment again. With a heavy sigh, Lulu turned about and entered the house.

"Oh, it's so lonesome for me here all by myself!" she said half-aloud.

But there was no one near enough to hear her, and she went back to her tasks, trying to forget her troubles in study — an effort in which she was for the time partially successful.

CHAPTER TENTH

"I HOPE THERE IS nothing serious ailing dear mamma," Violet said rather anxiously to herself, as the carriage rolled swiftly on toward Ion. "There was really nothing in her note to indicate it, but she has never been one to complain of even a pretty serious ailment. She is not old yet; we may hope to keep her with us for many, many years. But then she is so good—so ripe for heaven!" A silent prayer went up to God that the dear mother might be spared for many years to help others on their pilgrim way, especially her children and grandchildren. "For, oh, how we need her!" was the added thought. "What could we ever do without her—the dear, kind, loving mother to whom we carry all our troubles and perplexities, sure of comfort, the best of advice, and all the help in her power to give. Dear, dear mamma! Oh, I have never prized her as I ought!"

It was only the previous evening that Mrs. Travilla herself had learned that she was assailed by more than a trifling ailment. What seemed to her but a slight one, causing discomfort and at times quite a good deal of pain she had been conscious of for some weeks or months. But she had not thought it necessary to speak of it to anyone.

About the time of her return home, however, there had been a very decided increase in her suffering, which at length led her to confide her trouble to her cousin and family physician, Dr. Arthur Conly. She had learned from him that it was far more serious than she had supposed, and that in fact her only escape from a sure and speedy death lay in submission to a difficult and dangerous surgical operation.

Arthur told her as gently and tenderly as he could—assuring her that there was more than a possibility of a successful result. The surgery would bring relief from her suffering and prolong her life for many years.

His first words—showing her ailment as so much more serious than she had ever for a moment supposed it to be—gave her a shock at the thought of the sudden parting from all her dear ones—father, children, and grandchildren. Yet, before he had even finished, she was entirely calm and composed.

"And what would death be but going home?" she said. "Home to the mansions Jesus my Savior has prepared for those He died to redeem, and to the dear ones gone before, there to await the coming of those who will be left behind for a little while. Ah, it is nothing to dread or to fear, for 'I know that my Redeemer liveth.'"

"And yet, Cousin Elsie," Arthur returned with ill-concealed emotion, "how you could not be spared by any of those who know and love you. Even I should feel it an almost heartbreaking thing to lose you out of my life—to say nothing of your father, children, and grandchildren."

"Yes, I know, dear cousin, and I shall not hesitate to do or bear all that holds out a hope of prolonging my days here upon earth. Otherwise, I should feel that I was rushing into the Master's presence unbidden, and that without finishing the work He has given me to do here.

"Nor would I be willing to so pain the hearts of those who love me. I am ready to submit at once to whatever you deem necessary or expedient. But, ah, my dear father! How distressed he will be when he learns all that you have just told me! I wish he might be spared the knowledge till all is over. But it would not do. He must be told at once, and—I must be the one to tell him."

"That will be very hard for you, dear cousin. Would it not be better—" Arthur began, but paused, leaving his sentence unfinished.

"It will come best from me, I think," she returned with a sad sort of smile. "But when?"

"Day after tomorrow, if you will. I think you would prefer to have the trial over as soon as possible?"

"Yes, I think it will save both me and all those concerned from some of the suffering of anticipation, if you can make it suit your convenience."

"Perfectly," he answered. "There are only a few preparations to be made, and I do not want to long contemplate doing what must be a trial to so many whom I love."

Their talk had been in her boudoir. He lingered but a few moments longer, then went down to the drawing room.

"Uncle," he said in a low aside to Mr. Dinsmore, "I have just left Cousin Elsie in her boudoir, and she wishes to see you there."

"She is not well, Arthur?" asked the gentleman with a slightly startled look, as he rose from his easy chair and the two passed into the hall together.

"Not very, uncle," came the doctor's sad reply. "She has been consulting me upon the matter, and there is something she wishes to say to you at once, sir."

Mr. Dinsmore paled to the very lips. "Don't keep me in suspense, Arthur. Let me know the worst, at once," he said with almost a groan. "Why has anything been hidden from me—the father who loves her better than his life?"

"I have been as ignorant as yourself, uncle, till within the last half-hour," replied the doctor in a patient, deeply sympathizing tone. "It is astonishing to me that she has been able to endure so much for weeks or months past without a word of complaint. But do not despair, my dear uncle. The case is by no means hopeless."

"Tell me all, Arthur. Hide nothing, nothing from me," Mr. Dinsmore said with mingled sternness and entreaty, hastily leading the way from the other side of the hall and closing the door against any chance intruder.

Arthur complied, stating the case as briefly as possible and laying strong emphasis upon the fact that there was reason to hope for, not spared life alone, but entire and permanent relief.

"God grant it!" was the old gentleman's fervent, half-agonized response. "My darling, my darling, would that I could bear all the suffering for you! Arthur, when—when must my child go through the trial which you say is—not to be escaped?"

"We have agreed upon day after tomorrow, uncle. She and I both wish to have it over."

Only a few minutes later, Mr. Dinsmore passed quietly into his daughter's boudoir, where he found her alone. She was lying on a lounge, her eyes closed and her countenance, though deathly pale, perfectly calm and peaceful.

He bent down and touched his lips to the white forehead. Then as the sweet eyes opened and looked up lovingly into his, "Oh, my darling, idol of my heart," he groaned, "would that your father could himself take the suffering that I have just learned is in store for you."

"Ah, no, no, my dear, dear father, I could not bear that," she said, putting an arm about his neck. "Suffering and danger to you would be far harder for me than what I am now enduring or expecting in the near future. Arthur has told you all?"

"Yes, kindhearted and generous fellow that he is, he felt that he must spare you the pain of telling it yourself, my dear."

"Yes, it was very, very kind," she said. "Dear papa, sit down in this easy chair, close by my side, and take my hand in yours while we talk together of some matters that need to be settled before — before I am called to go through that which may be the end of earthly life for me."

Then, in response to the anguished look in his face as he bent over her with another silent caress, "My dear father, I do not mean to distress you. Arthur holds out strong hope of cure and years of health and strength to follow. Yet surely it is but the better part of wisdom to prepare for either event."

"Yes, and I am sure you are fully prepared, at least so far as your eternal welfare is concerned, should you be called away. Our grief would be for ourselves alone."

"I am glad the choice is not left with me," she said in low, sweet tones after a moment's silence. "For your sake, papa, and that of my beloved children, I am more than willing to stay here on earth for many more years, yet the thought of being forever with the Lord—near Him and like Him—thrills my heart with joy unspeakable. Added to that is a great gladness in the prospect of reunion with the dear husband who has gone before me to that happy land. So I am not to be pitied, my dear father," she added with a beautiful smile. "And can you not rejoice with me that the choice is not mine but lies with Him whose love for us both is far greater than ours for each other?"

"Yes," he replied with emotion. "Blessed be His holy name that we may leave it all in His hands, trusting in His infinite wisdom and love and knowing that if called to part for a season, we shall be reunited in heaven, never again to be torn asunder."

"Yes, dear father. We cannot expect to go quite together, but when we are reunited there in that blessed land, never again to part, the time of separation will seem to have been very short—even as nothing compared to the long, the unending eternity we shall spend together.

"And, oh, what an eternity of joy and bliss, forever freed from sin and suffering, near and like our Lord, altogether pleasing in his sight, no doubts, no fears, the battle fought, the victory won. 'And there shall be no more curse, but the throne of God and of the Lamb shall be in it, and His servants shall serve Him. They shall see His face, and His name shall be in their foreheads. And there shall be no night there, and they need no candle, neither light of the sun, for the Lord God giveth them light, and they shall reign for ever and ever!'"

"Yes, my darling. Blessed be His holy name for the great and precious promises of His word, and I have not a doubt of your full preparation for either event. But, oh, that it may please Him to spare you to me as the light, comfort, and joy of my remaining days! Yet, should it please Him to take you to Himself—ah, I cannot, dare not allow myself to contemplate so terrible a bereavement," he added in low, anguished accents, as he bent over her, softly smoothing her hair with a tenderly caressing touch.

"Then do not, dear father," she said, lifting to his eyes full of ardent love and sympathy. "Try to leave it all with the dear Master, and He will fulfill to you his precious promise, 'As thy days, so shall thy strength be.' Has it not ever been the testimony of all His saints concerning His precious promises that not one faileth?"

"Yes," he said. "So will it ever be. By His grace I will trust and not be afraid for you, my beloved child, nor for myself, His most unworthy servant."

Then with an upward glance, "'Lord, increase our faith.' Oh, help us each to trust in Thee and not to be afraid, be the way ever so dark and dreary, remembering Thy gracious promise, 'I will in no wise fail thee, neither will I in any wise forsake thee.'"

"Sweet, sweet words, papa," she said tremulously, lifting to his eyes full of glad grateful tears.

"And those others, 'When thou passeth through the waters, I will be with thee; and through the rivers, they shall not overflow thee; when thou walkest through the fire, thou shalt not be burned; neither shall the flame kindle upon thee. For I am the Lord thy God, the Holy One of Israel, thy Savior.'

"Oh, what more could I ask? What have I to do with doubt or fear, since He is mine and I am His?"

"Only the physical pain," he said tenderly. "And Arthur tells me that with the help of anesthetics there will little or none of that sort of thing during the operation, but—"

"What may come afterward can be easily borne, dear papa," she said, as he paused, overcome by great emotion.

"My dear, brave darling! A more patient, resigned sufferer never lived!" was his moved, though low-breathed, exclamation.

A moment of silence fell between them, he leaning over and caressing her with exceeding tenderness. Then, "Papa," she said with a loving look up into his eyes, "I cannot bear to see you so distressed. Arthur holds out strong hope of cure and of a speedy and entire recovery. We may be spared to each other for many years if the will of God be so, but, surely it is my wisest plan to prepare for every possibility.

"I feel very easy about my dear children, most of them having already arrived at years of maturity and being comfortably settled in life—Edward and my two older daughters, at least. The others I can leave in the safest of earthly hands, even those of my dear and honored father, whose love for them is only secondary to my own, and for each one I have reason to hope that the good part has been chosen, which can never be taken away."

"I do indeed love them very dearly," he responded. "For their own sake, their father's, and most of all because they are the offspring of my own beloved child. Should I outlive her, they shall want for nothing their grandfather can do to make them happy."

"I know it, dear father, and I can leave them to your and their heavenly Father's care without a doubt or fear," she said with a gentle sigh over the thought of the parting with her darlings that might be so near.

She went on to speak of some business matters, then said, "I think that is all, papa. I do not care to make any alteration in my will, and, as you know, you and Brother Horace are my executors. Tomorrow I must have a little talk with each of my children, and then I shall be ready for Arthur and his assistants.

"I want all my children near at hand in case of an unfavorable result so that I am able to say a few last words, bidding them all farewell."

There was again a moment of silence, her father seeming too much overcome to speak. Then, she went on, "I think they must not be told tonight, that the younger ones need know nothing of the danger till the morning of the operation. I would spare them all the suffering of anticipation that I can. And were I but sure, quite sure, of going safely through it all, they should know nothing of it till afterward. But I cannot rob them of a few last words with their mother."

"My darling! Always unselfish, always thinking of others first!" Mr. Dinsmore said in moved tones, bending over and pressing his lips again and again to her pale cheek and brow.

"Surely almost any mother would think of her children before herself," she returned with a sweet, sad smile.

But just at that instant, childish footsteps were heard in the hall without, then a gentle rap on the door, and Walter's voice asking, "Mamma, may I come in?"

"Yes, my son," she answered in cheerful tones. In a moment he was at her side, asking, in some alarm and anxiety, "Mamma, dear, are you sick?" bending over her as he spoke and pressing ardent kisses upon cheek and lip and brow.

"Not very, mother's darling baby boy," she answered, lifting to his, eyes full of tender mother love.

"'Baby boy?'" repeated Walter with a merry laugh, gently smoothing her hair and patting her cheek lovingly while he spoke. "Mamma, dear, have you forgotten that I am eleven years old?"

"No, dear. But for all that you are still mother's dear, dear baby boy!" she said, hugging him close.

"Well, I shan't mind your calling me that, you dearest mamma," laughed Walter, repeating his caresses. "But nobody else must do it."

"Not even your own grandpa?" queried Mr. Dinsmore with a proudly affectionate smile into the bright, young face.

"I don't think you'd want to, grandpa," returned the lad. "Because you're always telling me I must try to be a manly boy. But I came up to remind you and mamma that it's time for prayers. Grandma sent me to do so and to ask if you could both come down now."

"You will not be going down, Elsie!" Mr. Dinsmore exclaimed in surprise, as his daughter made a movement as if to rise from her couch.

"Yes, papa," she returned. "I have been resting here for some hours and feel quite able to join the family now. I am not in pain at this moment, and Arthur said nothing about keeping to my room."

"Then I wouldn't, mamma," said Walter, slipping his hand into hers. "I'm sure Cousin Arthur's always ready enough to order us to keep to our rooms if there's any occasion. I'm glad he doesn't think you sick enough to have to do that."

His mother only smiled in reply, and taking her father's offered arm, she moved on in the direction of the stairway with Walter still clinging to her other hand.

Anxious looks and inquiries greeted her on their entrance into the parlor, where family and servants were already gathered for the evening service. But she parried them all with such cheery words and sweet smiles as set their fears at rest for the time.

But those of Edward were presently rearoused as — the younger members of the family and the servants having retired from the room — he noticed a look of keen, almost anguished anxiety, bestowed by his grandfather upon his mother, then that her cheek was unusually pale.

"Mother, dear, you are not well!" he exclaimed, hastily rising and going to her.

"No, not quite, my dear boy," she replied, smiling up at him. "But do not look so distressed; none of us can expect always to escape all illness. I am going back to my room now and, though able to do so without assistance, will accept the support of the arm of my eldest son, if it is offered me."

"Gladly, mother dear, unless you will let me carry you, which I am fully able to do."

"No, Ned," she said laughingly, as she rose and put her hand within his arm. "The day may possibly come when I shall tax your young strength to that extent, but it is not necessary now. Papa, dear," turning to him, "shall I say goodnight to you now?"

"No, no," Mr. Dinsmore answered with some emotion. "I shall step into your rooms as it is the on the way to my own."

"I, too," said Mrs. Dinsmore. "Perhaps you will let me play the nurse for you."

"Thank you very much, mamma. In case your kind services are really needed, I shall not hesitate to let you know. And I am always glad to see you in my rooms."

"Mother, you are actually panting for breath!" Edward exclaimed when they were halfway up the stairs. "I shall carry you," and taking her in his arms as he spoke, he bore her to her boudoir and laid her tenderly down on its couch. "Oh, mother dear," he said in quivering tones, "tell me all. Why should your eldest son be shut out from your confidence?"

"My dear boy," she answered, putting her hand into his, "can you not rest content till tomorrow? Why should you think that anything serious ails me?

"Your pale looks and evident weakness," he said. "And grandpa's distressed countenance as he turns his eye on you, and the unusually sober, serious look of Cousin Arthur as I met him passing out of the house tonight. He had been with you, had he not?"

"Yes, my son, and that you and your sisters should know all tomorrow or the next day. It is only for your own sake I would have had you spared the knowledge till then."

"Dearest mother, tell me all now," he entreated. "For surely no certainty can be worse than this dreadful suspense."

"No, I suppose not," she replied in sorrowful tones, her eyes gazing into his, full of tenderest mother love. Then in a few brief sentences she told him all.

"Oh, mother dear, dearest mother!" he cried, clasping her close. "If I, your eldest son, might but take and bear it all—the pain and the danger—for you, how gladly I would do so!"

"I do not doubt it, my own dear boy," she returned in moved tones. "But it cannot be. Each of us must bear his or her own burden, and I rejoice that this is mine rather than that of my dear son. Do not grieve for me; do not be too anxious; remember that He whose love for me is greater than any earthly love appoints it all, and it shall be for good. 'We know that all things work together for good to them that love God.' Blessed, comforting assurance! And how sweet are those words of Jesus, 'What I do thou knowest not now; but thou shalt know hereafter!'"

"Yes, dearest mother!" he said with emotion. "And for you it will be all joy, the beginning of an eternity of bliss, if it shall please Him to take you to Himself, but, oh, how hard it will be for your children to learn to live without you! I will hope and pray that the result may be your restored health and a long and happy life."

For some moments he held her in a close embrace, then, at the sound of approaching footsteps in the hall without, laid her gently down upon her pillows.

"Keep it from Zoe for tonight, if possible," she said softly. "Dear little woman! I would not have her robbed of her night's rest."

"I will try, mother dear," he said, pressing his lips again and again to hers. "God grant you sweet and refreshing sleep, but do not for a moment hesitate to summon me if there is anything I can do to relieve you, should you be in pain, or to add in any way to your comfort."

She gave the desired promise, and he stole softly from her room. But he did not join his wife till some moments of solitude had enabled him so to conquer his emotion that he could appear before her with a calm and untroubled countenance.

Mr. and Mrs. Dinsmore passed into the boudoir as he left it. Rose had just learned from her husband of his talk that evening with Dr. Conly and what the physician had told him of his daughter's condition and the trial awaiting her in the future.

Rose was full of sympathy and so overcome at the thought of the trial she must so soon pass through that she could scarcely speak.

They clung to each other in a long, tender embrace, Rose shedding tears, Elsie calm and quiet.

"You will let me be with you, dear Elsie?" she said at last. "Oh, how willingly I would help you bear it if I could!"

"Dear mamma, how kind you are and have always been to me!" exclaimed the low, sweet voice. "Your presence will be a great support while consciousness remains, but after that I would have you spared the trial.

"Don't fear for me. I know that it will all be well. How glad I am that should I be taken you will be left to comfort my dear father and children. Yet I think that I shall be spared. Arthur holds out a strong hope of a favorable termination.

"So, dear father," turning to him and putting her hand in his, "be comforted. 'Be strong and of a good courage!' Do not let anxiety for me rob you of your needed rest and sleep."

"For your dear sake, my darling, I will try to follow your advice," he answered with emotion, as in his turn he folded her to his heart and bade her goodnight.

CHAPTER ELEVENTH

THE NEXT MORNING found Mrs. Travilla calm and peaceful, even cheerful, ready for either life or death. She was up at her usual early hour, and Rosie and Walter, coming in for their accustomed half hour of Bible reading with mamma, found her at her writing desk just finishing a note to Violet.

"Dear mamma," exclaimed Walter in a tone of delight, "you are looking so much better and brighter this morning. I was really troubled about you last night lest you were going to be ill. You were so pale, and grandpa looked so worried."

"Grandpa is always easily frightened about mamma if she shows the slightest indication of illness," said Rosie. "As indeed we all are, because she is so dear and precious—our very greatest earthly treasure.

"Mamma dearest, I am so rejoiced that you are not really sick!" she added, dropping on her knees beside her mother's chair, clasping her arms about her, and kissing her with ardent affection.

"I, too," Walter said, taking his station on her other side, putting an arm round her neck, and pressing his lips to her cheek.

She returned their caresses with words of mother love, tears shining in her eyes at the thought that this might prove almost her last opportunity.

"What do you think, Rosie?" laughed Walter. "Mamma called me her baby boy last night, me, a great fellow of eleven. I think that must make you her baby girl."

But Rosie made no reply. She was gazing earnestly into her mother's face. "Mamma, dear," she said anxiously, "you are not well! You are suffering! Oh, what is it that ails you?"

"I am in some pain, daughter," Elsie answered in a cheerful tone. "But Cousin Arthur hopes to be able to relieve it in a day or two."

"Oh, I am glad to hear that!" Rosie exclaimed with a sigh of relief. "Dearest mamma, I do not know how I could bear to have you very ill."

"Should that trial ever come to you, daughter dear, look to God for strength to endure it," her mother said in sweetly solemn accents, as she gently smoothed Rosie's hair with her soft, white hand and gazed lovingly into her eyes. "Do not be troubled about the future, but trust His gracious promise: 'As they days, so shall they strength be!' Many and many a time has it been fulfilled to me and to all who have put their trust in Him."

"Yes, mamma, I know you have had some hard trials, and yet you always seem so happy."

"You look happy now, mamma. Are you?" asked Walter a little anxiously.

"Yes, my son, I am," she said, smiling quite affectionately upon him. "Now let us have our reading," turning over the leaves of her Bible as she spoke. "We will take the twenty-third Psalm. It is short, and it is so very sweet and comforting."

They did so, Elsie making a few brief remarks, especially on the fourth verse, which neither Rosie nor Walter ever forgot.

She followed the reading with a short prayer, and just at its close her father came in, and, sending the children away, spent alone with his daughter the few minutes that remained before the ringing of the breakfast bell.

This was something very unusual for her, and, joined to an unusual silence on the part of their grandfather, accompanied by a sad countenance and occasional heavy sigh, and similar symptoms shown by both Grandma Rose and Edward, excited surprise and apprehension on the part of the younger members of the household.

Family worship, as was the rule, followed almost immediately upon the conclusion of the meal, and Mr. Dinsmore's feeling petition on behalf of the sick one increased the alarm of Rosie and Zoe.

Both followed Edward out upon the veranda, asking anxiously what ailed mamma.

At first he tried to parry their questions, but his own ill-concealed distress only increased their alarm and rendered them all the more persistent.

"There is something serious ailing mamma," he said at length. "But Cousin Arthur hopes soon to be able to relieve her. The cure is somewhat doubtful, however, and that is what so distresses grandpa, grandma, and me. Oh, let us all pray for her, pleading the Master's precious promise, 'If two of you shall agree on earth as touching anything that they shall ask, it shall be done for them of my Father which is in heaven.'

"Mamma has sent for my sisters Elsie and Violet. She wants as many of her children and grandchildren near her as possible, but Harold and Herbert have to be left out because, being so far away, there is no time to summon them."

"Oh, Ned," cried Rosie in an agony of terror, "is--is mamma in immediate danger? What—what is it Cousin Arthur is going to do?"

"A—surgical operation is—he says, the only—only thing than can possibly save her life, and—he hopes it will."

"But he isn't certain? Oh, mamma, mamma!" cried Rosie, bursting into an uncontrollable fit of weeping and sobbing.

Zoe was sobbing, too, Edward holding her in his arms and scarce able to refrain from joining with her. At that moment the Fairview carriage drove up, and Elsie Leland, alighting therefrom, quickly came in among them, asking in alarm, as she saw their tear-stained, agitated faces, "What ever is the matter? Oh, is mamma ill?"

Then Edward's story had to be repeated to her, and shortly afterward to Violet, who, with her children, arrived a little later.

They, too, seemed almost overwhelmed with their great distress at the news.

"Can we go to her?" Violet asked, and Mrs. Dinsmore, who had just joined them, replied, "Not yet. Your grandpa is with her, and he wishes to have her to himself for awhile."

"Oh. Oh, I hope he will not keep us long away from her, our own, own dear mother!" exclaimed Rosie with a fresh burst of tears and sobs.

"I think not long, Rosie, dear," Mrs. Dinsmore replied soothingly, putting an arm around the weeping girl as she spoke and smoothing her hair with gently caressing hand. "Your mamma will be asking for you all presently. She has said that until the danger is past, she wants you all near enough to be summoned to her side in a moment."

"And I—we all—know she is ready for any event," Elsie Leland said in trembling, tearful tones.

"Yes, and I believe God will spare her to us for years to come in answer to our prayers," remarked Mrs. Dinsmore in cheerful, hopeful accents.

Walter had gone out onto the grounds at the time the older ones repaired to the veranda, and Gracie, with Violet's little ones, had joined him there on alighting from the carriage that had brought them from Woodburn.

The four now came running in and Walter, noticing the looks of grief and anxiety on the faces of the older people, asked anxiously, "What's the matter, folks?" Then he added quickly, "Oh, I hope mamma is not worse! Is that it, grandma?" His query was not answered, for at that moment Dr. Conly's carriage came driving up the avenue. All crowded about him as he alighted and came up the steps into the veranda. That, however, was nothing new for he was a great favorite, being not only their relative, but their trusted and valued physician.

"You have come to see mamma?" Mrs. Leland asked. "Oh, Cousin Arthur, do be frank with us! Do tell us plainly what you think of her case."

"It is a serious one, Cousin Elsie, I will not deny that," the doctor replied, a very grave and concerned look on his face as he spoke. "And yet I have strong hope of complete recovery. So do not any of you give way to despair but unite together in prayer for God's blessing on the means used."

"Can I see her now, Aunt Rose?" he asked, turning to Mrs. Dinsmore.

"I think so," she replied, leading the way and the doctor following, while the others remained where they were, waiting in almost silent suspense.

To them all it seemed a long, sad day. One at a time they were admitted to a short interview with their mother, in which she spoke with each one as though it might be her last opportunity, the burden of her talk being always an earnest exhortation to a life hid with God in Christ—a life of earnest, loving service to Him who had died to redeem them from sin and eternal death.

She was very cheerful and spoke hopefully of the result of the operation, yet added that, if it proved fatal and in a way to leave her neither time nor strength for these last words, she must speak them now. But they need not despair of seeing her restored to health and given many more years of sweet companionship with her loved ones.

Walter, as the youngest, took his turn last.

For many minutes he could do nothing but sob on his mother's breast. "Oh, mamma, mamma," he cried, "I cannot, cannot do without you!"

"Mother knows it would be hard for her baby boy at first," she said, low and tenderly, holding him close to her heart. "But some day you would come to mamma in that happy land where there is no parting, no death, and where sorrow and sighing shall flee away—the land where 'the inhabitants shall not say I am sick;' the land where there is no sin, no suffering of any kind, and God shall wipe away all tears from our eyes.

"My darling, my little son, there is nothing else mother so desires for you as that you may be a lamb of Christ's fold, and I have strong hopes that you already are. You know that Jesus died to save sinners; that He is able to save to the uttermost all that come unto God by Him; that you can do nothing to earn salvation, but must take it as God's free unmerited gift; that Jesus says 'Him that cometh to Me I will in no wise cast out.' All this you know, my son?"

"Yes, mamma dearest," he sobbed. "Oh, how good it was of Him to die that cruel death that we might live! Yes, I do love Him, and He won't be angry with me because I'm almost heartbroken at the thought of maybe having to do without my dear, dear mother for many years. Oh, mamma, mamma, how could I live without you?"

"It may please the dear Lord Jesus to spare you that trial, my darling boy," she said. "I know that He will, if in His infinite wisdom He sees it to be for the best.

"And we must just trust Him, remembering those sweet Bible words, 'We know that all things work together for good to them that love God.' Leave it all with Him, my darling, feeling perfectly sure that whatever He orders will be for the best, and that, though we may not be able to see it so now, we shall at the last."

"But, mamma, I must pray that you may be cured and live with us for many, many years. It will not be wrong to ask Him for that?"

"No, not if you ask in submission to His will, remembering that no one of us knows what is really for our highest good. Remember His own prayer in His agony there in the garden of Gethsemane, 'Father, if thou be willing, remove this cup from me: nevertheless, not my will, but thine, be done.'

"He is our sublime example, and we must strive to be equally submissive to the Father's will. Remember what the dear Master said to Peter, 'What I do thou knowest not now; but thou shalt know hereafter.'"

"Mamma, I will try to be perfectly submissive to His will, even if it is to take you away from me. But, oh, I must pray, pray, pray as hard as I can that it may please Him to spare your dear life and let me keep my mother at least till I am grown to be a man. It wouldn't be wrong, mamma?"

"No, my darling boy, I think not—if with it all you can truly, from your heart, say, 'Thy will, not mine, be done.'"

⚜ ⚜ ⚜ ⚜ ⚜

When Captain Raymond followed his wife and little ones to Ion, he found there a distressed household, anxious and sorely troubled over the suffering and danger of the dearly beloved mother and mistress. Violet met him on the veranda, her cheeks pale and showing traces of tears and her eyes full of them.

"My darling!" he exclaimed in both surprise and alarm. "What ever is the matter?"

He clasped her in his arms as he spoke, and dropping her head upon his shoulder, she sobbed out the story of her mother's suffering and the trial that awaited her on the morrow.

His grief and concern were scarcely less than her own, but he tried to speak words of comfort to both her and the others to whom the loved invalid was so inexpressibly dear. He spoke kind words to the beloved invalid also when, like the rest, he was accorded a short interview.

Yet he found to his admiring surprise that she seemed in small need of such service—so calm, so peaceful, so entirely ready for any event was she.

Finding his presence a source of strength and consolation, not only to his young wife, but to all the members of the stricken household, he remained till after tea. But then he returned home for the night, principally for Lulu's sake—he not being willing to leave the child alone, or nearly so, in that great house.

CHAPTER TWELFTH

THE DUTIES OF THE schoolroom had filled up the rest of the morning for Lulu, so occupying her mind that she could give only an occasional thought to the sad fact that she was in disgrace with her father.

Then came dinner, which she took in the dining room, feeling it lonely enough with the whole family absent. Immediately after that, a music lesson filled another hour, and that was followed by an hour of practice on the piano.

Then Alma wanted her again, and then, knowing it was what her father would approve, she took her usual exercise about the grounds. After that, she prepared her lessons for the next day.

But all the time her heart was heavy with her consciousness of the fact that "papa, dear papa" was displeased with her, and she felt that there could be no happiness for her till she had made her peace with him.

"Oh," she sighed again and again, "will he never, never come, that I may tell him how sorry and ashamed I am."

But when teatime came he was still absent, and that meal also had to be taken alone.

She did not linger at the table. On leaving it, she went into the library where a wood fire blazed cheerfully on the hearth, for the evenings were now quite cool, and settling herself in an easy chair, she listened for the sound of his coming.

She was too much disturbed and too anxious to read or work, so she sat doing nothing but listening intently for the sound of horse's hoofs or carriage wheels on the drive without.

"Will he punish me?" she was asking herself. "I believe I want him to, for I'm sure I richly deserve it. Oh, there he is at last! I hear his voice in the hall!" and her heart beat fast, as she sprang up and ran to meet him.

He was already at the door of the room when she reached it.

"Papa," she said humbly and with her eyes on the carpet, "I—I'm very, very sorry for my naughtiness this morning. I have obeyed you—asked Alma's pardon—and—please, dear papa, won't you forgive me, too?"

"Certainly, dear child," he said, bending down to press a kiss upon her lips. "I am always ready to forgive my dear children when they tell me they are sorry for having offended and are ready to obey."

He led her to the easy chair by the fireside, which she had just vacated, and seating himself therein, drew her to a seat upon his knee.

"Papa, I'm so sorry, so very sorry for my badness, so ashamed of not being obedient to such a dear, kind father," she said, low and tremulously, blushing painfully as she spoke. "Please, I want you to punish me well for it."

"Have I not already done so, daughter?" he asked. "I doubt if this has been a happy day to you."

"Oh, no, indeed, papa! I soon repented of my badness and looked everywhere for you to tell you how sorry I was and ask you to forgive me. But you were gone and so I had to wait. The day has seemed as if it would never end, though I've been trying to do everything I thought you would bid me do if you were here."

"Then I need add no further punishment," he said, softly caressing her hair and cheek with his hand.

"But, please, I want you to, because I deserve it and ought to be made to pay for such badness. I'm afraid if I'm not, I'll just be bad again soon."

"Well, daughter," he replied, "we will leave that question open to consideration. I see you have books here on the table, and we will now attend to the recitations."

Her recitations were quite perfect, and he gave the deserved meed of praise, appointed the tasks for the next day, then drawing her to his knee again, said, "It does not seem to me necessary, daughter, to inflict any further punishment for the wrong doings of this morning. You are sorry for them, and you do not intend to offend in the same way again?"

"Yes, I am sorry, papa, and I don't mean to behave so any more. Still, I'd feel more comfortable, and surer of not being just as bad again in a few days or weeks, if you'd punish me. So please do."

"Very well, then, I will give you an extra task or two," he said, taking up her Latin grammar. "I will give you twice the usual lesson in this. Then, not as a punishment, but for your good, I want you to search out all the texts you can find in God's Holy Word about the sinfulness of anger and pride and the duty of confessing our faults, not only to Him, but to those whom we have injured by them."

Opening the family Bible that lay on the table close at hand, "Here is one in Proverbs," he said. "'He that covereth his sins shall not prosper, but whoso confesseth and forsaketh them, shall have mercy.'"

Then turning to the New Testament, he read again, "'Therefore, if thou bring thy gift to the altar, and there rememberest that thy brother hath aught against thee, leave there thy gift before the altar, and go thy way; first be reconciled to thy brother, and then come and offer thy gift.'"

"That is in Matthew," he said, "and here in the Epistle of James," again turning over the leaves, "we read perhaps the plainest direction of all on the subject, 'Confess your faults one to another, and pray one for another that ye may be healed.'"

"But, papa—" she paused, hanging her head, while a vivid blush suffused her cheeks.

"Well, daughter, what is it? Do not be afraid to let me know all your thoughts. I want you always to talk freely to me. I want my children to act intelligently, doing right because they see that it is right, and not merely because papa commands it."

"Please, don't be angry with me, papa, but, it did seem to me a sort of degradation to have to ask pardon of a—a woman who has to work for her living like Alma," she said with some hesitation, blushing and hanging her head as she spoke.

"I am very sorry to hear such sentiments from a daughter of mine," he returned in a gravely concerned tone and a slight sigh. "It is wicked pride, my child, that puts such thoughts in your head.

"And who can say that there may not come a time when you too will have to work for your living? The Bible tells us riches certainly take to themselves wings and fly away."

Again turning over the leaves, "Here is that passage—in the twenty-third chapter of Proverbs, fourth and fifth verses: 'Labor not to be rich; cease from thine own wisdom. Wilt thou set thine eyes upon that which is not? For riches certainly make themselves wings; they fly away as an eagle toward heaven.'

"And how little are they really worth, while we have them? 'Riches profit not in the day of wrath,' we are told in the Holy Book. And it says a great deal of the folly and sinfulness of pride; particularly in this book of Proverbs." Turning over the leaves he read here and there, "'When pride cometh, then cometh shame; but, with the lowly is wisdom.' 'Pride goeth before destruction, and a haughty spirit before a fall. Better is it to be an humble spirit with the lowly, than to divide the spoil with the proud.' 'Proud and haughty scorner is his name who dealeth in proud wrath.' 'A man's pride shall bring him low: but honor shall uphold the humble in spirit.' 'The fear of the Lord is to hate evil: pride, and arrogancy, and the evil way and the froward mouth, do I hate.'"

There was a moment of silence, then Lulu said humbly, tears starting to her eyes as she spoke, "Papa, I did not know—at least I never though about it—that pride was so wicked."

"Yes," he said, "the Bible tells us that every one proud in heart is an abomination to the Lord, that God resisteth the proud, but giveth grace unto the humble; there is much in the Bible against pride and in favor of humility. If we are all sinners, worthy of nothing good at the hands of God, what have we to do with pride?"

"Papa, when I say my prayers tonight I will ask God to take away all the wicked pride out of my heart. Won't you ask Him, too?"

"I will, my darling, as I have already, very many times, and I hope you have not neglected to ask Him to forgive your wrong thoughts, feelings, and actions of this morning?"

"I have asked for that, papa, and I will again," she replied quickly.

They were silent again for a little while, the captain looking as if his thoughts were far away. Lulu was studying his face with eyes that presently filled with tears.

"Papa," she said low and tremulously, "you look so sad. Is it all because you are grieved over my naughtiness, sir?"

"No, daughter, not at all. Indeed I was hardly thinking of that at the moment, but of the grief, sorrow, and anxiety at Ion."

"What about, papa?" she queried with a startled look. "Oh, I hope nothing bad has happened to Gracie, Mamma Vi, or our little ones?"

"No. I am thankful that all is right with them, but dear Grandma Elsie is in a very critical condition. I cannot tell you exactly what ails her, but she has been suffering very much for months, keeping it to herself till yesterday, when she told it all to Cousin Arthur and learned from him that nothing but a difficult and dangerous surgical operation could save her life.

"That is to be performed tomorrow, and, whether she lives or dies, it will relieve her from the dreadful agony she is enduring, for no one who knows her can doubt that she is one of God's dear children. Death would certainly be a gain to her, but a sad loss to all of us."

Before he had finished Lulu's face was hidden on his shoulder, and she was weeping bitterly.

"Oh, papa," she sobbed, "I'm so, so sorry for her, dear, dear Grandma Elsie! Isn't she frightened almost to death?"

"No, daughter. She is very calm and peaceful, ready to live or die as God's will shall be, grieving only for those who love her so dearly and find it difficult to be reconciled to the thought of losing her. Her efforts are all to comfort them. She has set her house in order and seems quite ready for either life or death.

"But we will pray—you and I—as the others are praying, that if God's will be so, she may live and go in and out before us for many years to come."

"Yes, papa. Oh, I am glad that we may ask our kind heavenly Father for everything we want! Poor Mamma Vi! How her heart must ache! And is she going to stay at Ion now, papa?"

"Yes, certainly till her mother is out of danger or forever done with sin and suffering. Gracie and our two little ones will stay, too, so that Gracie may amuse the others and keep them in the grounds or a part of the house so distant from Grandma Elsie's room that their noise will not disturb her."

"And you and I will stay on here, papa?"

"Yes, I must be here a good deal of the time to oversee my workmen, and I shall want my dear eldest daughter to be my companion and helper in various ways, for I know she loves to be such to her father," he added, pressing his lips to her cheek.

"Indeed I do, papa! Oh, thank you for letting me!" she exclaimed, lifting her head and showing eyes shining through tears. "I'd rather be here with you than anywhere else, my own dear, dear father!" putting her arms about his neck and hugging him close. "Only," she added, "I'd like to see

Gracie and the others for a little bit every once in a while if I may.'

"Yes, you shall," he said, returning her embrace. "Perhaps I may be able to take you over there for a short visit almost every day. And in the meantime we may hope that lessons and the dressmaking will go on prosperously."

"Are you going to spend your nights here at home with me, papa?" she asked with a wistful, pleading look.

"Yes, dear child. I could not think of leaving you alone, nor would your Mamma Vi wish me to do so while she has both her brother and grandfather near her, to say nothing of the women, children, and servants. You will have me close at hand every night and the greater part of the day."

"Oh, I am so glad and thankful!" she said with a sigh of relief. "I don't think I should be exactly afraid, because God would be with me, but it is so delightful to have my dear earthly father, too. May I sleep in Gracie's room to be nearer to you?"

"Yes, and with the door open between it and mine, so that if you want anything in the night you will only need call to me and I will come to you at once.

"Now, if there are any more questions you would like answered, let me hear them."

"There is something I'd like to say, papa, but I'm—almost afraid."

"Afraid of what, daughter?" he asked, as she paused in some embarrassment and with a half pleading look into his eyes.

"That you might think it saucy and be displeased with me."

"Do you mean it so, daughter?"

"Oh, no, indeed, papa!"

"Then you need not be afraid to let me hear it."

"Papa, it is only that I—I think if you had talked to me this morning, when you called me to you, about the wickedness of being too proud to ask Alma's pardon, and reasoned with me as you did a little while ago about it all, I—I'd have obeyed you at once. You know you do almost always show me the reasonableness of your commands before, or when, you lay them upon me."

"Yes, my child," he said in a kindly tone. "I have done so as a rule and I should have in this instance, but that I was much hurried for time. That will sometimes happen, and you and all my children must always obey me promptly, whether you can or cannot at the moment see the reasonableness of the order given. Is your estimation of your father's wisdom and his love for you so low that you cannot trust him thus far?"

"Oh, papa, forgive me!" she exclaimed, putting her arms about his neck and laying her cheek to his. "I do hope I'll never, never again hesitate one minute to obey any order from you. I know you love me and that you are very wise and would never bid me do anything but what I ought."

"Certainly never intentionally, daughter. Surely your father, who is so many years older than yourself, should be esteemed by you as somewhat wiser."

"Oh, papa, I know you are a great, great deal wiser than I," she said earnestly. "How ridiculous it seems to think of anybody comparing my wisdom with yours! I know I'm only a silly little girl, and not a good one either, and it would be a sad thing to have a father no wiser or better than myself."

CHAPTER THIRTEENTH

THE MORNING OF THAT very critical day found Grandma Elsie as calm and cheerful as she had been the previous evening, though every other face among the older members of the family showed agitation and anxiety. Her daughters, Elsie and Violet, were with her almost constantly during the early hours, doing everything in their power to show their devoted affection and make all things ready for the surgeons and their assistants. Her father and his wife also gave their aid and loving sympathy, while Edward and Zoe attended to all necessary arrangements elsewhere, occasionally snatching a moment to stand beside the dear sufferer and speak words of love and hope.

Rosie and Walter were each allowed one short interview in which they were clasped in her arms and a few loving, tender words spoken that both she and they felt might be the last.

Captain Raymond came a little earlier than the doctor. Lester was already there, and each young wife found the presence of her husband a comfort and support while, in an adjoining room, they waited in almost agonizing suspense to hear that the operation was over and what the result was.

They were a silent group, every heart going up in strong crying to God, that, if consistent with His holy will, the dear mother might be spared to them.

The united petition was granted. Mrs. Dinsmore presently came to them, her face radiant with joy and hope. "It is over," she said. "Successfully over, and the doctors say that with the good nursing she is sure to have she will soon be restored to perfect health."

The communication was received with tears of joy and thankfulness.

"It will certainly be strange indeed if she lacks anything the most devoted nurses can do for her," remarked Mr. Leland.

"I should think so, with three daughters, two sons, and as many sons-in-law, to say nothing of father and mother," remarked Violet with a tearful smile. "Levis, you will spare me to her as long as I am needed?"

"Certainly, my love," he replied without a moment's hesitation. "There is nothing we could refuse or grudge to our beloved mother at this, or indeed, at any time."

"Oh, grandma, may we go to her now?" queried Rosie and Walter in a breath.

"I think not yet, dears. She must be kept very, very quiet," was the gently spoken reply. "I know it would be a joy to both you and her to meet and exchange a few words, but it might be a risk for her. I know you would rather deny yourselves the gratification than do anything to increase her suffering, to say nothing of endangering her precious life."

"Oh, grandma, neither of us would be willing to do that for the wealth of the world!" exclaimed Rosie with starting tears.

"No, indeed!" cried Walter. "It is very hard to refrain, but we would not injure our mother for the world—our dear, dear mother!"

"I am sure of it," said Grandma Rose, smiling kindly upon him. "And now, Walter, would not you and Rosie like to go over to Fairview and carry the good news to Eva and Gracie? They are there with the little ones, and I know would be very glad to hear that your dear mother is over the worst of her trial."

"I am going there for Gracie, Elsie, and Ned to take them home to Woodburn for a while," said Captain Raymond. "If you two would like it, I will take you both with me, leave you there, bring you back here, or carry you on to Woodburn, as you may prefer."

"Thank you, sir," said Rosie. "I will be pleased to go as far as Fairview with you, but not on to Woodburn at this time, because I do not feel at all sure that mamma may not be taken worse. So I shall not stay long away from home."

Walter's reply was to the same effect, and as the captain's carriage and horses were already at the door, the three were presently on their way to Fairview.

Gracie and Evelyn were rejoiced to see them, and having been in great anxiety about their dear "Grandma Elsie," felt much relieved by the news of her which they brought.

The captain was in some haste to return to Woodburn, and Rosie and Walter, finding they wanted to stay a while with Evelyn and their sister Elsie's children, decided to walk back to Ion—the distance being none too great for either their strength or enjoyment.

Home and Sister Lu held strong attractions for Gracie, Elsie, and Ned, and they were full of delight as papa lifted them into the carriage and took his seat beside them.

"Et Ned sit on oo knee, papa," pleaded the baby, and he was at once lifted to the desired place.

"Papa's dear baby boy," the captain said, smoothing his curls and smiling down into the pretty blue eyes. "How glad Sister Lulu will be to see you, Elsie, and Gracie!"

"And we'll be just as glad to see her, papa," said Gracie. "I know it's not very long since we came away from our own dear home and Lu, but it does seem a long time."

"Isn't Lulu tired of doing without us, papa?" asked Elsie.

"I think she is," he replied. "At all events I know she will be very glad to see you. It is nearly dinner-time now," he added, looking at his watch. "So we will go directly home. But this afternoon I will take you all for a nice, long drive, then leave you little ones at Ion and take Lulu home again."

Lulu had been busy all morning attending to her studies, her practice on the piano, the demands of the dressmaker, and taking her usual exercise about the grounds. She was out in them now, watching for the coming of her father, eager to see him and to hear how it was with dear Grandma Elsie.

Presently she heard the sound of the carriage wheels on the road, then in another minute the vehicle turned in at the great gates and came rapidly up the drive, little Elsie calling out from it, "Lu, Lu, we've come!"

"Have you, Elsie? Oh, I'm so very, very glad!" she called in reply.

The carriage had stopped, Lulu bounded toward it, and her father, throwing open the door, helped her in. Hugs and kisses and laughter followed, so glad were the happy children to meet again after even so short a separation.

In another minute the carriage drew up before the entrance to the mansion, and the captain and his joyous troop alighted. Dinner was ready to be served, and as soon as hats and other outer garments had been disposed of the merry little party gathered about the table. Mamma was missed but it was very pleasant to all to find themselves there with their fond father and each other. Lulu's fears for dear grandma Elsie had been much relieved by the report of the success of the surgeons, so that she was as light-hearted and merry as the little ones.

Immediately after dinner, while the little ones took their afternoon nap, she recited her lessons, doing so in a manner that drew hearty commendation from her father, who was always glad to be able to bestow it. Then, knowing it would be a joy to her to do them, he called upon her for some of the little services she was accustomed to render him.

These attended to, "Now, daughter," he said, "you may dress yourself nicely for a drive. I am going to take you and your little brother and sisters for a pretty long one. Then I will drop them at Ion, and you and I, after a call of a few minutes to hear how Grandma Elsie is, will drive home together."

"Oh, how pleasant that will be, papa! How good you always are to every one of us children!" she exclaimed, giving him an ardent kiss then running away to do his bidding.

A merry, happy time the children had, and on reaching Ion, the little ones were ready for their supper and bed. The older ones were full of joy on learning that their loved Grandma Elsie was as comfortable and doing as well as possible under the circumstances. The captain and Lulu spent a quiet half-hour with the Ion family and Violet, then departed for Woodburn.

As the carriage started, the captain put an arm around Lulu, drew her close to him, and smiling affectionately down into her face, said: "How glad I am to be able to keep one of my loved flock with me!"

"And, oh, how glad I am that I'm the one, you dear, dear papa!" responded the little girl, returning his loving look and smile. Then, with a sigh, "I think there are some fathers who wouldn't be very fond of even their own child if she were so often ill-tempered and disobedient. Papa, I've been thinking all day that you didn't punish me half so severely as I deserved for my naughtiness the other day."

"I would rather err on that side than the other, daughter," he said in tender tones. "And I hope your future behavior will be such as to prove that the slight punishment inflicted was all-sufficient."

"I hope so, indeed, papa," she answered earnestly. "But if I am disobedient and ill-tempered again soon, you will be more severe with me, won't you? I really want you to, that I may improve."

"Yes, daughter, I think I must," he replied a little sadly, but then after a moment's silence, he went on again. "I expect to pay a little visit to Max in January, and if my eldest daughter has been a good and obedient child—" he paused, looking smilingly at her.

"You will take me with you, papa?" she cried breathlessly. "Oh, how I should like it! Ah, I do hope I shall not be so bad that you will have to leave me behind."

"No, I hope not. I want to take you — to share the pleasure of my dear, eldest daughter will double it for me, and if neither bad conduct on your part, nor anything else happens to prevent, you shall go with me, Lulu."

"Oh, thank you, dear papa!" she exclaimed, her cheeks glowing and her eyes sparkling with delight. "You are so good to me that I just hate myself for ever doing anything to vex or grieve you."

"My dear child," he said with emotion, "be more watchful, careful, and prayerful; fight more earnestly and determinately the good fight of faith, ever looking to God for help, for only so may you hope to gain the victory at last, and to be able to say, 'in all things we are more than conquerors through Him that loved us.'"

"I will try, papa," she said, tears starting to her eyes. "But, oh, it is such a hard fight for anybody with a temper like mine. Please help me all you can by praying for me and punishing me, too, papa, whenever you see that I need it."

"I will do all I can for you, my darling, in every way," he replied. "But as I have often told you, Lulu, the hardest part of the conflict must inevitably be your own.

"Cling close to Jesus, and cry to Him every day and every hour for help, for only by His all-powerful assistance can we hope to win holiness and heaven at last."

"I will try, papa; I will indeed," she said. "I am, oh, so glad and thankful that He will let me cling to Him and that He promises His help to those who ask Him for it."

"Yes, He says, 'In Me is thine help,' and having His help, what can harm us since He is the Lord who made heaven and earth?"

Again a few moments of silence, then Lulu said, "Papa, you have often told me I inherit my temper from you, and though I could never believe it if anybody else had told me, I have to believe you because I know you will always speak the truth. But how did you ever conquer it so completely?"

"By determined effort, at the same time looking to God for help," he replied. "And only by the same means can I even now keep it under control."

"And you think I can learn to control mine if I use the same means?"

"I do. God, our kind heavenly Father, is as able and as willing to help you as me."

"Yes," she said thoughtfully. "And if I don't choose to try hard enough, at the same time praying earnestly for help, I deserve to be punished by my earthly father, and I do really hope he always will punish me till he has taught me to be as patient and self-controlled as he is," she added, nestling closer to him and slipping a hand into his. "Papa, I often wonder why I wasn't made as patient and sweet-tempered as Gracie. She doesn't seem to have any temper at all to fight."

"No. But she has her own peculiar temptations, some of which your firmer, braver nature knows nothing. Each must battle with her own faults and failings, looking to God for help in the hard struggle. To God, who, the Bible tells us, 'will not suffer you to be tempted above that ye are able; but will with the temptation also make a way to escape that ye may be able to bear it.'"

"It is a precious promise, papa," she said with thoughtful look and tone. "I am glad you reminded me of it. It makes me feel less discouraged about trying to conquer my besetting sins."

"In the first chapter of Joshua," replied her father, "the Lord says to him three times, 'Be strong and of a good courage,' the last time adding, 'be not afraid, neither be thou dismayed; for the Lord thy God is with thee whithersoever thou goest.' And that blessed assurance of the constant, sustaining presence of our God each one of His children may take to him or herself."

"What a comfort, papa!" she exclaimed. "Oh, the Bible is such a blessing! I do feel sorry for all the people who have none."

"Yes," he responded, "they are greatly to be pitied, and those who have dared to take it from others will have much to answer for in the day of judgment, as will those also who, having it themselves, make no effort to supply it to such as have it not.

"Ah, here we are at our own home!" he added, as the carriage drew up before the entrance.

"And such a sweet home it is!" she responded, as he threw open the door, sprang out, and took her in his arms.

"Yes," he said, "so I think and am glad my little girl appreciates it. There," setting her on her feet, "run in, daughter, and make yourself ready for the tea table."

She obeyed and presently the two were seated cozily at a little round table in the family breakfast room, greatly enjoying their tea, broiled chicken, and waffles.

"Papa," remarked Lulu, as she poured out his second cup, "I'm sorry for you that you have only me for company, but I do enjoy being—once in a while—all the family you have at home."

"Do you now, Lulu?" he returned with quite a good-humored little laugh. "Well, I am glad to have you contented and happy, and I can't deny that I should feel very lonely tonight without the pleasant companionship of my dear, eldest daughter. What do you want to do this evening? How shall we spend our time alone together?"

"I have my lessons to learn, you know, papa."

"Ah, yes, and I must write some letters. And after that perhaps you may find a bit of sewing to do, while your father reads aloud something that will be both interesting and instructive to his little girl."

"Yes, sir. I have some work on hand for our Dorcas Society, and though I rather dislike sewing, I shall not mind doing it while listening to your reading," she answered, smiling brightly up into his face.

"Ah! Then that is what we will do," he said, returning her smile.

⚘ ⚘ ⚘ ⚘ ⚘

"Well, daughter, has it been a pleasant evening to you?" he asked, when the time had come for the goodnights to be said.

"Indeed it has, papa," she replied, giving him an ardent hug. "Oh, I am so glad you didn't let me go to Ion with the others but kept me at home with you. I do hope that I'll remember after this that you always know and do the very best thing for me, and that I'll never grow ill-tempered and rebellious, as I was the other day."

"You think you can trust your father after this, even without being told his reasons for all he does and requires?"

"I hope so, papa, and indeed, indeed I'm very much ashamed of my rebellious feelings and don't intend to indulge in them any more!" she added with a remorseful look up into his face.

"Try to keep that resolution, dear child," he said. "Now goodnight and pleasant dreams. May He who neither slumbers nor sleeps have you in His kind care and keeping. But if you want your earthly father you have only to call out or run to him."

CHAPTER
FOURTEENTH

LULU'S FIRST THOUGHT upon awakening the next morning was of dear Grandma Elsie. "I wonder," she said to herself, "if papa has not been asking news of her through the telephone. Oh, I hope she is getting well!"

Hurrying through her dressing, she was ready to run to meet her father when presently she heard his steps in the hall without.

"Good morning, papa," she cried. "Have you heard from Ion how Grandma Elsie passed the night?"

"Yes," he said, bending down to give her a good morning kiss, "she passed a very comfortable night and is thought to be doing as well as possible. Mamma Vi and our little ones are all right also. I have just talked with your mamma on the telephone."

"Oh, I am glad! How nice it is that we can talk in that way to the folks at Ion and the other places where Mamma Vi's relations live!"

"Yes, a telephone is really a blessing under such circumstances. I am more reconciled to being at some short distance from my wife and little ones than I could be without such means of communication."

They went down to the library together, and seating himself, he drew her to his knee, saying pleasantly, "You are the youngest child at home with me, and I think I must have you here. I hope you will never think yourself too old to sometimes sit on your father's knee."

"No, papa, I'm sure I never shall while you are willing to let me," she replied, putting an arm round his neck and gazing lovingly into his eyes.

They chatted for a few minutes, then the breakfast bell rang, and presently they were again seated at the little round table from which they had eaten last night's supper, Lulu pouring the coffee with a very grownup air, while her father filled her plate and his own with the tempting viands.

"What a lovely, delightful home we have, papa!" she remarked, as she handed him his cup. "I do really think that with such a father and such a home I ought to be the best girl in the world. I do mean to try to be."

"I have no doubt you do, daughter, and I have seldom had occasion to find serious fault with you in the last year or more, so that I am by no means in despair of seeing you gain control of that troublesome temper that has caused so much unhappiness to both you and me."

"Oh, thank you for saying it, papa!" she returned with a bright and joyous smile. "I'm determined to try my best to be as good as possible, both to please you and to earn that visit to Annapolis. I think it will be very delightful. How pleased Max will be to see us, especially you."

"I think he will. Ah, here comes the mailbag!" as a servant entered with it.

"Oh, I hope there's a letter from Max," Lulu said, as her father opened the bag and took out the contents—papers, magazines, and letters.

"Yes, here is one from our dear boy," he said, singling out a letter and hastily tearing it open.

He read it first to himself, then aloud to her—a bright, cheery, boyish, affectionate epistle such as they were accustomed to received from Max's pen.

They talked it over together while they finished their breakfast, then returned to the library, where, as usual, Christine, Alma, and the servants being called in, the captain led the family devotions, reading a portion of Scripture and engaging in prayer.

"Are you going immediately to Ion, papa?" asked Lulu, when again they were alone together.

"No," he replied. "I have some matters to attend to here while you are preparing your lessons. After hearing them, if your recitations and conduct have been satisfactory, I intend to take you with me to the village, where I have to make some business arrangements. Then we will drive to Ion, spend a little time there, then come home, probably bringing your little sisters and brother with us as we did the other day, returning them as before to your Mamma Vi, just in time for supper and bed, and coming home alone together."

"Oh, I like that, papa!" she exclaimed. "And is it what you intend to do every day?"

"Every day while your Grandma Elsie is so ill that the noise might disturb her. I think it will be a relief to your Mamma Vi to have them here a good deal of the time, till her mother is better."

"I suppose so, papa. At the same time it is very pleasant for us—they are such darlings!"

"So you and I think," he said with a smile. "Now go to your lessons, daughter."

At Ion, Grandma Elsie lay quietly sleeping, her three daughters watching over her with tenderest care and solicitude. Scarce a sound was to be heard, either within doors or without, save the distant lowing of cattle, the twittering of birds, and the gentle sighing of the wind in the treetops. Family and servants moved with cautious tread, speaking seldom and that with bated breath, lest they should disturb her who was so dear to all hearts.

To Walter it seemed very hard to be shut out of mamma's room, and he sat on the veranda watching for the coming of Cousin Arthur—to petition for admittance, if only for a moment, just to look at her and come away again.

Cousin Arthur had been with her through the night, had gone away early in the morning, and was expected back again soon.

The half hour spent in watching and waiting seemed very long indeed to the little lad, but at last, oh, joy, there was Cousin Arthur's sulky turning in at the gates. Then it came swiftly up the avenue, and Walter rose and hastened to meet the doctor as he alighted.

"Cousin Arthur!" he cried aloud but in subdued tones. "They've shut me out of mamma's room, and I just don't know how to stand it any longer. Mayn't I go in, if it's only for a minute, to get one look at her dear face? I won't speak to her or touch her if you say I must not, but, oh, I don't know how to endure being kept away from her altogether."

The little fellow's tones were tremulous, and his eyes filled with tears as he spoke.

Dr. Conly felt for the child, and laying a hand kindly on his head, said cheerfully, "Don't be downhearted, my boy; your mother will be well enough in a few days, I hope, to stand quite an interview with her youngest son. Perhaps it may do for you to go in for a moment this morning. You may come upstairs with me and wait in the hall till I see how she is. If I find her well enough to stand a peep from her boy, you shall go in for a minute, provided you will promise to be cheerful and not to speak unless you have the doctor's permission."

"Oh, I'll promise to do anything you bid me, if you'll only let me see her," returned Walter in eager tones, and he followed the doctor with noiseless tread through the hall and up the broad stairway.

Reaching his mother's door, he paused and waited outside while the doctor went quietly in.

His patient seemed to be asleep, but she opened her eyes and smiled up into his face as he reached the bedside.

"Dear cousin," he said, low and tenderly, "are you feeling quite easy now?"

"Quite so," she answered in low, sweet tones. "All is going right, I think. Is it not?"

"Yes, so it would seem. You are the best of patients, and with the abundance of good nursing you are sure to have, I think we will soon have you about again. But," glancing around upon her three daughters, "she must be kept very quiet, neither talking nor being talked to much more than is absolutely necessary.

"However, I am going to allow Walter a moment's sight of his mother. As he is your baby boy, you may, if you choose, speak half a dozen words to him," he added, addressing himself directly to the patient.

Then stepping to the door, he beckoned to Walter and led him to the side of the bed.

"There, laddie, you may tell her how dearly you love her, but nothing more."

"Mamma, dear, darling mamma! I couldn't begin to tell it!" Walter said, low and tremulously, just touching his lips to her cheek.

"Mother's darling boy!" was all she said in response, but the soft eyes looking into his spoke volumes of mother-love.

"Don't cry, Walter, my man," his cousin said, as he led him out into the hall again. "You have behaved so well that I think you may be allowed another interview tomorrow. I hope you will see your mother up and about again in perhaps a fortnight from this. You must pray for her healing to the Great Physician, as we all are doing. Pray in faith, for you know the Bible tells us He is both the hearer and the answerer of prayer."

"Oh, I will! I do!" sobbed the child. "I'm so glad there are so many others asking for her, too. The Bible says Jesus promised that His Father would grant what two or three agreed together to ask for."

"Yes. Pray for your mother, believe God's promises, and be happy in the expectation that she will get well. With a mind at rest, interest yourself in your studies and sports. That's my prescription for you, my lad. Now go and take it like a good boy," added the doctor with a smile, as he turned and reentered the sickroom.

"A funny prescription, and not so bad to take," laughed Walter to himself, as he wiped away his tears and hastened to the schoolroom to attend to his lessons.

"Nobody here but myself," he sighed, as he crossed the threshold. "It's rather lonesome, but I'll do the best I can. It's what mamma would advise."

CHAPTER FIFTEENTH

GRACIE HAD GONE over to Fairview with her little brother and sister, accompanied by their nurse, Mamma Vi having told her she might learn her lessons there. If Evelyn cared to hear her recite, that would answer very well.

Evelyn was entirely willing, and they had just finished a few minutes before the carriage from Woodburn came driving up the avenue, bringing Gracie's father and sister Lulu.

They had already paid a call at Ion, and now they had come to make a short one at Fairview and pick up Gracie, little Elsie, and Ned.

"Papa!" shouted the two little ones, running to meet him as he came up the steps onto the veranda and holding up their faces for a kiss.

"Papa's darlings!" he responded, taking them in his arms to hug and kiss them, then letting them go to give Gracie her turn.

"Is my feeble little girl quite well this morning?" he asked in tender tones.

"Yes, papa, thank you," she replied, giving him a vigorous hug. "I am, oh, so glad to see you! Have you come to take us—Elsie and Ned and me— home for a while again?"

"I have," he said, returning her hug. "I can't have mamma at present, as her mother needs her, but my dear babies I need not do without."

"Am I one of them, papa?" asked Gracie with a smile. "I'm almost eleven, but I don't mind being one of your babies, if you like to call me that." His only reply was a smile and a loving pat on her cheek, for the two little ones were tugging at his coat and coaxing for a drive.

"Why, Elsie and Ned, you haven't kissed me yet," said Lulu. "Gracie and Eva did while you were exchanging hugs and kisses with papa, and I think it's my turn now."

"I love you, Lu," cried Elsie, leaving her father for a moment to throw her arms round Lulu's neck in a hearty and loving embrace. Ned quickly followed suit, then running to his father again, renewed his request for a drive in the carriage.

"Yes, my son, you shall have it presently," said the captain. Then he proposed to Evelyn that she and her two little cousins should join the party for a short drive in another direction, before he would take his own children home to Woodburn.

His invitation was joyfully accepted, and in a few minutes they had all crowded into the captain's carriage and were driving down the avenue.

The little ones were very merry, and the captain did not check their mirth. He was, in fact, in very good spirits himself, because thus far Grandma Elsie's cure had progressed so favorably. It continued to do so from that time until in two weeks she was able to be up and about a part of every day. Violet returned to Woodburn, though daily, when the weather permitted, she drove over to Ion and spent an hour or more with her mother.

Quite frequently the captain drove her over himself, and leaving her there, went on into the village to attend to some business matter, calling for her on his return.

On one of the occasions of his return, going into the parlor, he found there his wife, her mother, eldest sister, and grandparents in very earnest conversation with the doctor.

When the customary greetings had been exchanged, Grandma Elsie said to him with a smile, "Captain, these good people seem to have leagued together to send, or to take me, to Viamede to spend the winter. Cousin Arthur has given his opinion that a warmer climate than this would probably be of benefit just at this time."

"In which I presume he is quite right, mother," returned the captain. "Surely there is no difficulty in the way?"

"Nothing insurmountable," she replied.

"But we want someone to go on in advance and see that everything is in order for mamma's comfort," said Violet, giving her husband a look that was half entreating, half one of confident assurance that he would deny nothing to her or her loved mother that it was at all in his power to bestow.

"That, I think, would certainly be the better plan," he returned pleasantly. "And if no one more competent than myself is to be had, and it suits my wife to accompany me, my services may be considered as offered."

Hearty thanks were at once bestowed upon him by all present.

But he disclaimed all title to them, saying, "I now have everything in order at Woodburn, so that I may feel quite easy in leaving it for even a protracted stay. To get a view of Viamede will be a new and doubtless very pleasant experience to me with wife and little ones along. My daughters can go on with their studies under my tutelage there as well as at home, and my intended visit to Max can be paid before starting for the far South. I only fear," he added with a pleasant glance at Mrs. Leland, "that I may be offering to take upon myself a duty which is much to the taste of one of my brothers-in-law and might be better performed by one or both of them."

"No, captain," replied Mrs. Leland. "You need have no such fear, as neither of them is just now in a position to leave home, unless it were quite necessary for dear mamma's comfort."

"Then we will consider it settled that Violet and I are to go," said the captain, turning to her with a smile. "How soon can you be ready, my dear?"

"By the first of next week if my husband wishes to start by that time," returned Violet merrily. "Oh, I am quite delighted at the prospect of seeing Viamede again, and especially of doing so in company with you, Levis."

The captain considered a moment. "I would not like to disappoint Max," he said. "I think I must visit him next Saturday. But I will make necessary arrangements beforehand, and I think we may leave for the South by Wednesday morning of next week, if that will suit you, my dear?"

"Entirely," she said. "It will give me time enough to get everything ready without hurry or confusion."

So it was settled, everybody seeming to be well satisfied with the arrangement.

A little more time was spent in discussing plans, then the captain and Violet bade good-bye and set out on their return home.

"You are well pleased with the prospect of this visit to Viamede, Violet, my dear?" the captain said, as they drove rapidly along the familiar road.

"Oh, yes, indeed," she answered brightly. "Viamede is so lovely, a sort of earthly paradise I have always thought, and I am really delighted at the thought of showing it to you. Ah, I am quite sure, having your dear society there, I shall enjoy it more than ever!"

"Thank you, dearest," was his smiling response. "I am certainly pleased with the prospect of seeing that earthly paradise, particularly with you to share my enjoyment. And how pleased Lulu and Gracie will be, for I have often heard them speak of Viamede as even lovelier than Woodburn, which they evidently esteem a very delightful and lovely home."

"As it assuredly is," was Violet's smiling rejoinder. "I could not ask a lovelier, happier home than that which my husband—the very best and dearest of husbands—has provided for me. Oh, I often ask myself, 'Is there anybody else in all the wide world who has so much to be thankful for as I?'"

"Ah, that fortunate mortal is surely he who sits by your side at this moment, my darling," he answered in moved tones, taking her hand in his and pressing it affectionately.

But the carriage was turning in at the Woodburn gates, and presently the glad shout of little voices was borne to their ears on the evening breeze. "There it is! Papa and mamma have come home!"

A joyously tumultuous greeting followed, the little flock gathering about them as they alighted— talking, laughing, dancing around them, and claiming their attention and their caresses.

Elsie and Ned pleaded for a ride, and Gracie and Lulu seemed not averse to sharing it. So there was a hasty bundling up in capes, hoods, cloaks, and shawls. Papa piled them in, followed them, taking Ned on his knee, and away they went for a mile or more down the road, then back again, and were presently taking off their outdoor garments in the hall, mamma helping the little ones.

Then all gathered about the tea table with appetites that made everything taste very good indeed. Elsie and Ned were too busy to talk much, but Lulu and Gracie were unusually merry and mirthful, and their father indulged them in more than the usual chat and laughter that were neither rude nor boisterous.

Neither he nor Violet said anything of the new plans for the winter till the babies had had their evening romp and been taken away to bed. Violet, as usual, went with them, and the captain was left alone with Lulu and Gracie.

They were hanging lovingly about him as was their custom on such occasions, and he drew one to each knee, saying in low, tender tones, "My darlings! My precious little daughters! How rich I feel in the possession of my five dear children!"

"And how rich we feel with our dear, dear father—to say nothing of our dear, sweet Mamma Vi and the two darling babies!" responded Lulu, putting her arm about his neck and her lips to his.

"Yes, and our big brother, Maxie," added Gracie.

"Yes, I was just going to mention him," said Lulu. "I am both very fond and very proud of Max. I wouldn't swap him for any other body's brother that ever I saw—no, not even for all the nice brothers that Rosie has."

"Neither would I," said Gracie, "though I'm fond of them all."

"Papa, when is it that we are going to see Max?" queried Lulu. "Some time in January, I know you said, but will it be to spend New Year's with him?"

"No. Wouldn't you like to go sooner than that?" he asked, stroking her hair and looking down both lovingly and smilingly into her eyes.

"Oh, yes, indeed, papa! If it suits you to go and to take me," she answered eagerly. "It seems now a long, long while that I have been separated from Max, and the sooner I may go to see him the better. But have you changed your plans about it?"

"Yes," he replied. "I have something to tell you both, which will show you why and also prove pleasant news to you, I think."

Then he proceeded to tell them of the plans laid that afternoon at Ion, which made it necessary that, if he went to Max at all that winter, he must do so before the end of the week already begun.

His news that their winter was to be spent at Viamede was hailed with delight by both the girls.

"I am so glad!" cried Gracie, clapping her hands and smiling all over her face.

"I, too," exclaimed Lulu. "Viamede is so, so very beautiful, and to have you there with us, you dear papa, will make us — me anyway — enjoy it at least twice as much as I did before."

"Me, too," said Gracie. "The happiest place for me is always where my own dear father is with me," hugging him tight and kissing him again and again.

"My darlings! My precious darlings!" the captain said in response, caressing them in turn.

"I'm so sorry for poor Maxie," remarked Gracie presently, "That he can't see you every day, papa, as we do, and be kissed and hugged as we are and that he can't go to Viamede with the rest of us." She finished with a heavy sigh.

"Yes," her father said, "I am sorry for him, and for ourselves that he is not to be with us. But my dear boy is happy where he is, and I in the thought that he is preparing himself to do good service to our country and to be a valuable and useful citizen."

"And we are all ever so proud of him—our dear Maxie, but I'm glad I am not a boy. Women can be useful in the world, too, can't they, papa?"

"Yes, yes, indeed, my darlings. The world cannot go on without women, any more than without men. Both are necessary, and the one sex to be as much honored as the other. I hope and trust my daughters will all grow up to be noble, true-hearted, useful women, always trying to do earnestly and faithfully the work God has given them to do."

"I hope so, indeed, papa!" responded Lulu in an earnest, thoughtful tone. "If I know my own heart I do want to be a very useful woman when I'm grown up—a useful girl now—serving God with all my might. But, oh, I do so easily forget and go wrong!"

"Yet I can see very plainly that my dear little girl is improving," her father said, softly smoothing her hair with his hand. "And I'm sure—for the Bible tells us so—that if you fight on, looking to God for help, you will come off conqueror and more than conqueror in the end."

"Yes, papa. Oh, I am so glad the Bible says that!"

There was a moment's silence. Then Gracie said with a sigh and a voice full of tears, "Oh, I do so wish I could see Maxie before we go so far away from him! Papa, wouldn't they let him come home for just a little while?"

"No, daughter. But how would you like to go with Lulu and me to pay him a little visit?"

"Oh, papa! So much if—if you think I won't be too tired to go on to Viamede so soon afterward."

"I really think you could stand the two journeys, coming so near together, now that you are so much stronger than you used to be and as you can lie and rest in the cars. We go by water from New Orleans. Don't you feel as if you could?"

"Oh, yes, papa, I feel almost sure I could!" she cried joyously.

"Then we will try it,' he said, hugging her. "You will have no packing to do—I am sure Mamma Vi and Lulu will be pleased to attend to all that for you—and the journey to Annapolis is not a very long or fatiguing one. So, should nothing happen to prevent, you shall make one of our little party to visit Max."

Gracie's eyes shone with pleasure, and Lulu exclaimed delightedly, "Oh, I am so glad, Gracie! It will double my pleasure to have you along. You needn't worry one bit about your packing of clothes or playthings, for I'm sure I can see to it all with Christine and Alma to help me, or even if I should have to do it all myself."

"Oh, thank you very much, Lu!" exclaimed Gracie. "You are just the very best sister that ever I saw! Isn't she, papa?"

"I think her a very good and kind sister, and it makes me a proud and happy father to be able to give her that commendation," he answered with a loving look down into the eyes of his eldest daughter.

Just then Violet reentered the room and a merry, happy hour followed, while plans and prospects were under discussion.

"Won't you excuse Gracie and me from lessons the rest of the time before we start for Viamede, papa?" asked Lulu coaxingly.

"No, daughter," replied the captain in a pleasant tone. "There is very little either of you will be called upon to do in regard to the preparations, so there is no occasion for you to miss lessons. You cannot study on the boats and cars — at least I shall not ask it of you. And when we get to Viamede, you will be glad of a little holiday to rest and run about, seeing everything that is to be seen, and all that will cause quite sufficient loss of time from your lessons."

"Oh, dear," sighed Lulu, "I think it must be so nice to be grown up and not have any lessons to learn."

"Ah, Lu," laughed Violet, "I am not so sure that grown up folks have no lessons to learn. In fact, I begin to have an idea that their lessons are not seldom more trying and wearisome than those of children."

"Yes, Mamma Vi," responded Lulu with a blush. "I'm sorry and ashamed of my grumbling. Papa, I'm determined I will be good and do cheerfully whatever you bid me. I have always, always found your ways the very best in the end."

"Of course, papa always knows far better than we do what is best for us," said Gracie, leaning lovingly up against him and smiling up into his face.

"Papa is very happy in having such loving and trustful little daughters," he said, passing his hand caressingly over Gracie's golden curls.

CHAPTER SIXTEENTH

IT WAS A MOST JOYFUL surprise to Max when, on the following Saturday, his father and sisters walked in upon him, as he left the dinner table full of life and pleasure at the thought of the half holiday that had just begun.

His standing and conduct had been such that he was entitled to leave, and the privlege to be able to spend it with these dear ones was most delightful.

A carriage had brought the captain and his little girls to the door, and they—father and children—took a long drive together, during which the tongues of Max and Lulu ran very fast.

Both she and Gracie thoroughly enjoyed Max's surprise on learning of the plans for the winter so soon to be carried out.

At first he seemed to feel rather badly at the thought that they would all be so far away from him, but he presently got over that. His father spoke of the letters he would receive from Viamede every day and how quickly the winter would pass, when all be coming home again, and some of them—certainly himself—making haste to pay a visit to the Academy to see their young cadet and learn what progress he was making in preparing for future duty in the naval service of his country.

At that Max's face brightened, and he said heartily, "And I shall try my best to have as good a report as possible ready for you, papa, that you may be proud and happy in your firstborn son. Ah, the thought of that does help me to study hard and try very, very earnestly to keep rules, so I may be an honor, and not a disgrace to the best of fathers."

"Yes, I am sure of it, my dear boy," the captain replied, laying his hand on the lad's shoulder, while the light of fatherly love and pride shone in his eyes. "I haven't a doubt that it is one of my son's greatest pleasure to make himself the joy and pride of his father's heart."

They drove back to the Academy just in time for Max to be ready to report himself at evening roll call, according to the rules, with which no one was better acquainted than the captain.

He and the little girls were to start on their return journey that evening, and their good-bye was said at the Academy door.

A very hard one it seemed to the little girls, hardly less so to Max and his father. The captain and his daughters went by boat, as it was less fatiguing for Gracie, and they reached home on Monday. The next day was a busy one to all, and Wednesday noon saw them on the cars, bound for New Orleans.

A day and night were spent in the city, and then they took the steamer for Berwick Bay.

The morning was both clear and bright, and the captain, Violet, and the children all sat upon the deck, greatly enjoying the breeze and the dancing of the waves in the sunlight, as the vessel cleared its port and steamed out into the gulf.

"Oh, it is so pleasant here!" exclaimed Gracie. "Just like summer, and see the beautiful rainbow in the water that the wheel throws up!"

"Oh, yes. It is so pretty, oh, so pretty!" cried little Elsie, clapping her hands in delight.

"Oh, so pitty!" echoed baby Ned.

"Take care, my little ones. I fear you may fall overboard," warned the captain. "Come and sit on papa's knee, and perhaps mamma will kindly tell us of all the lovely things we will see at Viamede."

They obeyed and were charmed with mamma's story of what she had done and seen at Viamede when she was a little girl, of dear grandma being once a baby girl in the very same house, how dearly all the old servants loved her, and how they mourned when she was taken away to live with her grandpa at Roseland.

The babies and even the older folks, not excepting papa himself, seemed deeply interested and more delighted than before that they were so soon to see the beloved Viamede.

At length Ned fell asleep, and little Elsie presently followed his example. The older people were then left to the quiet enjoyment of the lovely scenes through which they were passing—for they had now entered Teche Bayou. From that they pressed on, threading the way through lake and lakelet, past plantation and swamp, plain and forest, coming upon cool, shady dells carpeted with a rich growth of velvety grass and flowers of varied hue, shaded by magnificent trees—oaks and magnolias. Amid groves of orange trees they could see lordly villas, tall, white sugar houses and rows of cabins where the laborers dwelt.

"A beautiful, beautiful country," remarked the captain, breaking a prolonged silence.

"Quite up to your expectations, my dear?" queried Violet, glancing up at him, her eyes shining with pleasure. "I believe it rather exceeds them," he replied. "It is very, very lovely—indeed, an earthly paradise, so far as beauty can make it such."

"Papa, do you suppose you will know which is Viamede when you see it?" queried Lulu.

"I very much doubt it, daughter," he answered.

"Yes, sir. There it is, just coming into sight—the sugar house, at least, and yonder, a little beyond, is the great orange orchard."

"And it's just beautiful!" cried Gracie. "See, papa, the orange trees with their beautiful, glossy leaves, ripe and green fruit, and flowers all on them at once."

"And presently we will come to the beautiful lawn with its giant oaks, magnolia trees, velvety grass, and lovely flowers," exclaimed Lulu. "Oh, I am so much obliged to dear Grandma Elsie for inviting us to spend the winter here again!"

"Yes, it is very kind," her father said. "I hope my children will do nothing to mar the peace of the household and so distress Mamma Vi's dear mother."

"I do intend to be a very good girl, papa, and if I begin to be the least bit bad, I hope you'll stop it at once by punishing me well and making me behave myself," Lulu said in a low, earnest tone, speaking close to his ear.

"Dear child," he returned in the same low key in which she had spoken, "I have not the least doubt that you intend to be and do all I could ask or wish."

There was no time for anything more just then, for, as they were nearing their destination, baggage must be seen to and satchels and parcels gathered up.

Presently, the boat rounded to at the wharf, and in another minute greetings and embraces were being exchanged with the cousins, who, having been duly informed of the intended arrival, were gathered there to give both a cordial and delighted welcome to Violet, her husband, and children.

There were servants also, some few of the old and some new ones, each and all eager for a handshake and a few words of greeting from "Miss Wi'let and the cap'n and dere chillens," in which they were not disappointed.

In a few moments, the baggage had been landed and was being taken to the house, while ladies, gentlemen, and children followed, the newly arrived gazing delightedly upon the beauties of the place, the others asking many questions concerning Grandma Elsie and those of her family left behind—how they were in health and when they would come to Viamede.

"You will find the house in very tolerable order, I think, Vi," remarked Mrs. Keith. "Doubtless many little repairs and improvements are needed that Cousin Elsie may find everything in order when she comes. It was a good idea to get you and the captain to come a little in advance of the older folk and have everything in order for their reception."

"I think so," Violet said with a smile, "and that no better person than my honored husband could have been found to undertake that task."

"No more trustworthy one, I am sure, judging from his looks," remarked Isa. "I am delighted with his appearance, Vi. He is as noble-looking a man as ever I saw."

Violet flushed with pleasure. "And he is all that he appears to be, Isa," she said. "The better he is known the more highly he is esteemed."

A bountiful supper had been prepared for the travelers, and the others stayed and partook with them. But soon after leaving the tea table, they all bade a goodnight and went away to their own respective homes.

The Violet took her sleepy little ones upstairs to see them to bed, leaving the captain, Lulu, and Gracie on the veranda.

As usual, the two were hanging lovingly about their father, he seeming to enjoy it as much as they.

It was a beautiful moonlight night—warm and sweet with the breath of flowers. Away in the distance, beyond the wide-spreading lawn, they could see the waters of the bayou glittering in the moonbeams, and the soft plash of oars came pleasantly to their ears.

"Oh, isn't it just lovely here?" exclaimed Lulu, breaking a momentary silence. "Papa, did I at all exaggerate in telling you of the beauties of the place?"

"No, I think not," he replied. "It is certainly very lovely, and I hope we are going to have a happy winter here."

"I'm sure we will. I'm happy anywhere with you, my dear, dear papa," said Gracie, putting an arm round his neck and pressing her lips to his cheek.

"So am I," said Lulu, "unless I have been doing wrong, and papa is displeased with me. Oh, I do mean to try my very hardest to be good! And I'm sure it will be ever so much easier with you for my tutor, dear papa, than it was before, going to that horrid school and having to take music lessons from that Signor Foresti, who was so ill-tempered and struck me when I was trying as hard as I could to play my piece just right."

"Yes, daughter, I think it will be easier for you with the tutor who loves you and is loved by you," assented the captain, drawing her into a close, loving embrace. "We must see if a music teacher is to be had here, but I certainly will not try Signor Foresti again."

"Oh, I am glad to hear you say that, papa, though I never thought you would send me back to him again! I am, oh, so glad I belong to you instead of to anybody else."

"So am I," he responded with a happy laugh.

"And that I do, too, papa?" asked Gracie in a soft and pleading tone.

"Yes, yes, my own darling," he said, addressing her with great tenderness. "You are no less dear than your sister."

"How good of you, papa, for I'm not half so bright or pretty as Lu," she said, patting his cheek with her small, white hand.

"Why, Gracie!" exclaimed Lulu. "Whatever put such a thing as that into your head? You are far prettier and better, too, than I am. Isn't she, papa?"

"You must not ask me such hard questions," he returned laughingly, hugging them both up in his arms. "I really could not say that either is prettier or dearer to me than the other or that I love either more or less than I do each of the other three. The love differs somewhat in kind, but, I think, not at all in its intensity."

"Yes, papa; I suppose so," Lulu said thoughtfully. "For instance you must have quite a different sort of love for Max, who is almost old enough to take care of himself, and baby Ned, who is so very young and helpless."

Violet joined them at that moment, reported the babies fast asleep in the nursery, and consulted her husband as to what rooms they should occupy during their stay, saying her mother had kindly bade them please themselves in regard to that matter.

"Choose for yourself, darling," replied the captain. "I shall be entirely satisfied—only I should like to have these children close at hand with a door of communication between their room, or rooms, and ours, if that can be easily managed. We must be near the babies, of course."

"Yes, indeed! Near every one of our children," returned Violet brightly. "I could not be easy otherwise, any more than their father.

"But suppose I take you over the house, if you are not too tired. Tomorrow, you remember, is Sunday, and I could hardly wait till Monday, to say nothing of the curiosity that must be consuming you."

"Of course," returned the captain laughingly, as he rose and gave her his arm. "It will give me great pleasure to accompany you, if you are not too weary for such exertion."

"Not a bit," she said. "The trip on the boat was more restful than fatiguing—at least so far as concerned myself. May not Lulu and Gracie come, too?"

"If they wish; though I fear Gracie is too tired," he said with an inquiring glance at her. "If you would like to go, dear, papa will carry you up the stairs."

"Oh, then, I would like to, papa. I'm not so very tired," she answered eagerly.

"Then, of course, Lulu is not?" he said with a smiling glance at his eldest daughter.

"No, indeed, papa, and I'd dearly love to go along," she answered, taking Gracie's hand and with her tripping along in the rear, as he and Violet passed on into the wide hall.

They first inspected the rooms on the lower floor, lingering longest in the drawing room, where the many beautiful paintings and attractive pieces of statuary were housed.

"We cannot give them half enough time tonight," remarked Violet. "But fortunately, we have good reason to hope for many opportunities for your future inspection."

"Yes," the captain said, glancing at Gracie then at his watch. "Shall we not call in the servants and have prayers before going upstairs? It is not far from the usual time, and I see Gracie is growing weary quickly."

Violet gave a ready assent and led the way to the family parlor where her grandfather had been wont to hold that service.

The servants were summoned and came in looking pleased. The captain made the service short out of consideration for Gracie's weariness, though, indeed, he never thought it well to lengthen it so much as to risk making it a weariness to either children or servants.

A few directions in regard to securing doors and windows for the night and as to what should be done for the comfort of the family in the morning were given, and then he, Violet, and the little girls, having exchanged kindly goodnights with the servants, went up the broad stairway with the captain, according to promise, carrying Gracie in his arms.

Only a hasty survey of the upper rooms was taken that night, for all began to feel the need of rest and sleep. Apartments connected with each other and the nursery were selected for occupation, and soon all were resting peacefully in their beds.

CHAPTER SEVENTEENTH

THAT SWEET SABBATH morning dawned bright and clear. Lulu rose with the sun, and before he was an hour high, she was down on the veranda, gazing with delight upon the lovely landscape spread out at her feet.

So absorbed in its beauties was she that she failed to hear an approaching footstep, and she was aware of her father's presence only when he laid a hand gently on her head and, bending down, imprinted a kiss on her lips.

"An early bird as usual, my darling!" he said.

"Yes, like my father," she returned, twining her arms around his neck and holding him fast.

"Did you sleep well?" he asked, releasing himself and taking her hand in his.

"Oh, yes, indeed, papa! Did not you?"

"I did. I think we all did," he answered. "God has been very good to us. And what a lovely, lovely Sunday morning it is!"

"We can all go to church, can't we not, papa?" she asked.

"I think so," he said. "Would you like to walk down across the lawn to the water's edge with me, Lulu?"

"Oh, yes, indeed, papa," she cried delightedly. "It was just what I was wanting to do."

"It might be well for you to have a bit of something to eat first," he said. "Ah, here is just the thing!" as a servant approached with a waiter on which were some oranges prepared for eating in the way Grandma Elsie had enjoyed them in her young days.

"Thank you very much, Aunt Sally," the captain said, helping Lulu and himself. "You could have brought us nothing more tempting and delicious. Will you please carry some up to my wife?"

"I'se done it already, sah," replied the woman, smiling all over her face and dropping a curtsy. "Yes, sah. An' she say dey's mighty nice, jes like she hab when she's heah in dis place yeahs ago."

"Papa," remarked Lulu, as they presently crossed the lawn together, "I'm so glad to be here again and with you. It was a delightful place the other time, I thought, but, oh, it seems twice as pleasant now, because my dear father is with us!" She lifted her eyes to his face with a look of ardent affection.

"Dear child, it is a great pleasure for me to be with you and the rest," he returned, pressing affectionately the little hand he held in his. "And if you do not have a happier time than you had here before, it shall not be because your father does not try to make it so.

"But, my dear little daughter, remember you have the same spiritual foes to fight here as in other places. If you would be happy you must try to live very near to Jesus—to watch and pray lest you enter into temptation. Particularly must you be ever on your guard against that quick temper which has so often gotten you into trouble."

"Papa, I do intend to," she said with a sigh. "I am very glad I shall have you close at hand all the time to help me in the fight—for you do help me, oh, so often, dear papa!" Again she lifted her dark eyes to his face.

"I am very thankful that I can, my darling," he returned. "I feel that God has been very good to me in so changing my circumstances that I can be with you almost constantly to aid you in the hard task of learning to control the fiery temper inherited from me. Yet, as I have often told you, dear child, the hardest part of the fight must inevitably be your own, and only by the help of Him, who has all power in heaven and in earth, can you hope to conquer at last.

"I want you to feel that in your inmost soul, and to beware of self-confidence, which was, I think, the cause of your sad failure of a few weeks ago."

"Yes, papa," she said humbly. "I believe I had begun to feel that I was quite reformed, and so I did not watch and pray as constantly as I used to. Then almost before I knew it, I was in a passion with poor Alma."

"'When I am weak, then I am strong!' the apostle says," returned her father. "That is when we feel our weakness and trust in the strength of our Almighty Savior—of Him who has said, 'In me is thine help.' It is help, daughter, which is never refused to those who look humbly to Jesus for it."

"I am glad the Bible tells us that," she said.

They walked on in silence for a little, then Lulu said, "Papa, I asked Cousin Molly last night if Professor Manton still had his school at Oakdale. She said, 'Yes, is your papa going to send you there?' and I was so glad I could answer, 'No, ma'am, he is going to teach me himself.' Then Cousin Molly said, 'Oh, is he? I am sure that will be far pleasanter for you, dear. The professor is not very popular, and I hear his school grows smaller.'"

"Ah, then don't you think it would be only kind of me to put my eldest daughter there as a pupil?" asked the captain jestingly.

"Not to me, papa, I am sure," she answered, lifting to his smiling eyes that said as plainly as any words could have spoken that she had no fear that he would do any such thing.

"No, and I do not know what could induce me to do so," he returned. "So you need never ask it, but you must try to content yourself with the tutor who has had charge of your education ever since Woodburn became our home."

"I don't need to try, papa," she said with a happy laugh. "It's just as easy as anything. Gracie and I both think there was never such a more dear or kinder teacher than ours. Neither of us wants ever to have any other."

"Ah! Then we are mutually pleased. And now I think we should turn and go back to the house, for it must be near the breakfast hour." They found Violet, Gracie, and the little ones on the veranda, awaiting their coming, for breakfast was ready.

Morning greetings were exchanged, and all repaired to the breakfast room.

The meal proved a dainty one and was daintily served and enlivened by cheerful chat on such themes as were not unsuited to the sacredness of the day.

Family worship followed, and soon after, the family carriage was at the door ready to convey them to the church of which their Cousin Cyril was pastor.

The captain, Violet, and the two little girls, Lulu and Gracie, formed the deputation from that family, the two babies remaining at home in the care of their nurses, whom they had brought with them from Woodburn.

Cyril gave an excellent sermon, and at the close of the exercises, conducted a Bible class attended by nearly everyone belonging to the congregation.

The Viamede family remained to its close, held a little pleasant talk with the relatives from the parsonage and Magnolia Hall, then drove back to Viamede, reaching there just in time for dinner.

In the afternoon, the captain gathered his family and servants under the trees in the lawn, read and expounded a portion of scripture, and led them in prayer and the singing of several familiar hymns.

The evening was spent much as it would have been at Woodburn, and all retired early to rest.

Monday morning found them all in good health and spirits, entirely recovered from the fatigues of the journey, and ready for work or play.

"We don't have to learn and recite lessons today, papa, do we?" asked Lulu at the breakfast table. "I think you said we could have a day or two for play first, didn't you?"

"Yes, but I shall give you your choice of having that playtime now or taking it about a week hence, when you will have Rosie and Walter with you."

"May I choose, too, papa?" asked Gracie.

"Yes."

"Then I choose to wait for my holiday until the others are here to share it with us—for don't you suppose Grandma Elsie will let them, papa?"

"No doubt of it," he replied. "And what is your choice, Lulu?"

"The same as Gracie's, papa," she answered in bright cheerful tones. "Lessons are not bad to take with you for my teacher," she added laughingly. "You will leave us a good deal of time for running about and looking at everything, I'm sure."

"Besides an occasional drive or walk with mamma and papa," he supplemented with an approving smile. "The lessons shall not be long or hard today, so that you will still have some time for roaming about the grounds, and perhaps, if my pupils are very deserving, there may be a row on the bayou after dinner."

"Oh, how very, very delightful, papa!" they cried in a breath.

"I am glad you think so," he said, smiling on them. "There is nothing I enjoy more than giving pleasure to my wife and children," he said with an affectionate glance at Violet. "I hope such a little excursion will afford you pleasure, my dear?"

"Yes," she returned merrily. "I think even the children will hardly enjoy it more than I," she added laughingly. "I shall endeavor to earn my right to it by faithfully attending to housekeeping matters in the meantime."

"I don't believe there is any schoolroom here!" exclaimed Gracie, as if struck with a sudden thought.

"We will have to select one and get it ready before the others come," said Violet.

"For the present, my dressing room will answer very well," added the captain.

So thither the children repaired at the usual hour for the beginning of their studies.

It was at first a little difficult to fix their attention upon them, but with an earnest desire to do right and to please their dear father, they made very determined efforts and had their lessons very well prepared by the time he came to hear them.

It seemed to afford him pleasure to give the deserved meed of praise, and the young faces grew bright and gladsome under it. An hour was then given to writing and ciphering, and they were dismissed for the day.

"May we go out into the grounds now, papa?" asked Lulu, as she put up her books.

"Yes," he replied, "but keep near the house for the present, for it is near dinner time now."

"We will, papa," both little girls answered and hurried away.

They sported about the lawn till summoned to the house by the dinner bell, whose call they obeyed with alacrity, air and exercise having given them good appetites.

"My dear," the captain said to his wife near the conclusion of the meal, "you've had a busy morning. Can you afford to devote the afternoon to recreation?"

"Certainly, if you will share it," she replied. "Are we now to have that row on the bayou?"

"It is what I had planned, should my wife still feel inclined to go," he said.

"Ah! That will be very enjoyable I think. Perhaps there may be time afterward for me to drive over to the parsonage. I want a bit of chat with Isa about some household matters."

"Yes, I think you may have time for both," he returned. "An hour on the bayou will be sufficient for this first time. The carriage can be ordered to be waiting when we return, and you, if the plan suits your views, can drive over to the parsonage at once, have your talk, and be home again in season to pour out your husband's tea."

"That will do nicely, thank you, sir," she returned merrily. "I see I am not likely to lack for diversion with you at the head of affairs, so I think I shall try to keep you there as long as possible."

"I hope you will, Mamma Vi," said Lulu. "And anyway, I'm glad that when papa is about, he is the one that has control of me."

"So I have at least one willing subject," remarked the captain, looking not ill-pleased.

"Two, papa," said Gracie. "You can always count on me for one."

"I don't doubt it in the least, dear child," he said. "And now, as I see you have all finished your dinner and the boat is at the wharf, let us be going."

In a few minutes all were seated in the boat, and it was moving rapidly over the water; the children were very merry; and the parents were by no means disposed to check the manifestations of their mirth.

They found the carriage waiting when they landed.

"You are going with us, Levis?" Violet said inquiringly, as the captain handed her in.

"I should be very pleased to do so, my dear, but I have too many business letters calling for immediate reply," he said, lifting little Ned and then Elsie to a place by her side. "Lulu and Gracie, you would like to go with your mamma?"

"Yes, sir, if I may," Gracie answered with alacrity. But Lulu declined, saying, "I would much rather stay with you, papa, if I may."

"Certainly, dear child. I shall be glad to have you," he said with a pleased look. "But I fear you will find it dull, as I shall be too busy to talk to you or let you talk to me."

"But I can be with you and perhaps of some use waiting on you, papa."

"Perhaps so," he said. "You generally contrive to make yourself rather useful to your father in one way or another."

The carriage drove on, Lulu slipped her hand into his, and together they walked back to the house.

"I do hope I can find something to do that will help you, papa," she said, as they entered the library.

"I verily believe my dear, eldest daughter would like to carry all her father's burdens if she could," he said, laying his hand caressingly on her head. "But it wouldn't be good for me, my darling, to have my life made too easy."

"I am sure it wouldn't hurt you, papa, and I only wish I could carry all your burdens," she replied with an ardently affectionate look up into his face. "Isn't there something I can do now?"

"Yes," he replied, glancing at the table. "Here are papers, magazines, and letters—quite a pile. You may cut leaves and open envelopes for me. That will save me some time and exertion and be quite a help."

"Yes, sir. I'll be glad to do it all. But, oh, papa," and a bright, eager look came into her face.

"Well, daughter, what is it?" as she paused half-breathless with her new idea.

"Papa, couldn't I write some of the letters for you? Here is my typewriter that you so kindly let me bring along. I've learned to write pretty fast on it, you know, and wouldn't it be easier for you just to tell me the words you want said and let me put them down, than to do it all yourself with either it or your pen?"

"That is a very bright thought, daughter," he said, patting her cheek and smiling down upon her. "Lulu, I dare say that plan would shorten my work considerably."

"Oh, I shall be so glad if it does, papa!" she exclaimed. "There is nothing in the world I'd enjoy more than finding myself a help and comfort to you."

"I have found you both many a time, daughter," he responded, taking up and opening a letter as he spoke, while she picked up a paper cutter and fell zealously to work opening envelopes, laying each one close to his hand as she had it ready.

"Now, you may get your typewriter ready for work," he said presently. "Put in a sheet of this paper," taking some from a drawer in the table and laying it beside the machine, "date it, and in a moment I will tell you what to say."

He had already instructed her carefully in punctuation and paragraphing—spelling also. And with an occasional direction in regard to such matters, she did her work well.

She was full of joy when at the close of their business he bestowed upon her a judicious amount of praise and said that she had proved a great help to him, shortening his labor considerably.

"I think," he concluded, "that before long my dear eldest daughter will prove quite a valuable amanuensis for me."

"Papa, I am so glad!" she cried, her cheeks flushing and her eyes sparkling. "Oh, there is nothing else in the world that I enjoy so much as being a help and comfort to my dear, dear father!"

"My precious little daughter," he responded, "words cannot express the love your father feels for you. Now there is one letter that I wish to write in my own hand, and while I am doing that, you may amuse yourself in any way you like."

"May I read this, papa?" she asked, taking up a magazine close at hand.

"Yes," he said, and she went quietly from the room with it in her hand.

She seated herself on the back veranda, read a short story, then stole softly back to the library door to see if her father had finished his letter so that she might talk to him.

But someone else was there—a stranger she thought, though she did not get a view of his face.

She paused on the threshold, uncertain whether her father would wish her to be present at the interview. At the instant he spoke, apparently in reply to something his caller had said, his words riveted her to the spot.

"No," he said in stern tones, "had I been here my daughter would not have been sent back to your school. She was most unjustly and shamefully treated by that fiery little Italian, and you, sir, upheld him in it. When I am at hand no daughter of mine shall be struck by another man, or woman either, with impunity, and Foresti may deem himself fortunate in that I was at a distance when he ventured to commit so great an outrage upon my child."

Lulu waited to hear no more, but she ran back to the veranda, where she danced about in a tumult of delight, clapping her hands and saying exultingly to herself, "I just knew papa wouldn't have made me go back to that horrid school and take lessons of that brute of a man. Oh, I do wish he had been here! How much it would have saved me! If my father is strict and stern sometimes, he's ever so much better and kinder than Grandpa Dinsmore. Yes, yes, indeed, he's such a dear father! I wouldn't exchange him for any other, if I could."

Presently she suddenly ceased her jumping and dancing and stood in an intently listening attitude.

"Yes, he's going—that horrid professor! I'm so glad! I don't believe he'll ever trouble this house again, while papa is in it anyway," she said aloud.

Then running to meet her father as he returned from seeing the professor to the door, she threw her arms around him, exclaiming in a voice quivering with delight. "Oh, you dear, dear papa, I'm so glad, so glad to know that you wouldn't have made me go back to that horrid music teacher! I felt sure at the time that you wouldn't if you were here."

He heard her with a look of astonishment not unmixed with sternness.

"Oh, papa, please don't be angry with me!" she pleaded, tears starting to her eyes. "I didn't mean to listen, but I happened to be at the library door, as I was coming back to see if you were done writing that letter and I might be with you again, when you told Professor Manton that you wouldn't have sent me back to Signor Foresti, nor even to his school. It made me so glad, papa, but I didn't stop to hear any more. I ran away to the veranda again, because I knew it wouldn't be right for me to listen to what wasn't intended for me to hear."

He took her hand, led her into the library again, drew her to a seat upon his knee, and softly stroking back the hair from her forehead, said in kind, fatherly tones, "I am not displeased with you, daughter. I understand that it was quite accidental, and I am sure my little girl is entirely above the meanness of intentionally listening to what is evidently not meant for her ear. In fact, now that I think of it, I am not sorry that you know I did not, and do not now approve, of the treatment you received at that time. Yet that was the first time I had ever mentioned it to anyone, and I should be sorry to have your Grandpa Dinsmore know, or even suspect, how entirely I disapproved of what he thought best to do at the time. Can, and will, my little daughter promise to keep the secret—never mentioning it to anyone but me?"

"Yes, indeed, papa," she returned, looking up brightly into his face. "Oh, it's nice to be trusted by you and not even threatened with punishment if I disobey you!"

"I am happy to think that is not necessary," he said, drawing her into a closer embrace. "I believe my little girl loves her father well enough to do of her own free will what she knows he would have her do."

"Yes, indeed, papa," she answered earnestly. "And do you know it seems a great pleasure to have a secret along with you. But, papa, why did you write—after I had confessed it all to you—as if you were so much displeased with me that you couldn't let me stay any longer at Ion after you had found another place to put me?"

"My child, as I had put you under Grandpa Dinsmore's care, it was your duty to submit to his orders till I could be heard from in regard to the matter. You should therefore have gone back, not only to the school, but to the music teacher when he directed you to do so. You were disobeying both him and me in refusing, and you were also showing great ingratitude to the kind friends who were doing so much for you without your having the slightest claim upon them."

"Papa, I am very sorry and ashamed," she murmured low and tremulously, hanging her head and blushing deeply as she spoke. "I almost want you to punish me well for it even now."

"No, daughter, that account was settled long ago," he said in kindly, reassuring accents. "Fully settled, and I have no desire to open it again."

"But, papa," she sighed, "sometimes I do feel afraid I may get into a passion with somebody about something while we're here this winter with all the Ion folks, that — that I believe I want you to say you will punish me very severely if I do."

"My daughter," he said, "I want you to avoid sin and strive to do right, not from fear of punishment, but that you may please and honor Him whose disciple you are."

"Oh, yes, papa, I do want to for that reason and also to please and honor you — the best and dearest father in the world!" she concluded, putting her arms round his neck and laying her cheek lovingly to his. "But you will watch me and warn me and try to keep me from yielding to my dreadful temper?"

"Yes, dear child, I will, as I have promised you again and again, do all I can to help you in that way," he replied in tenderest tones.

Then, as the carriage wheels were heard on the drive without, he said, "Ah, your mamma and our little ones have returned," he said, putting her off his knee. Then, taking her hand, he led her out to the veranda to meet and welcome them home.

CHAPTER
EIGHTEENTH

"HAD YOU A CALL from Professor Manton, Levis?" asked Violet, as they sat together on the veranda that evening. "I thought so because he passed us as we were coming home, and he was looking very glum."

"Yes, he was here this afternoon," replied the captain.

"In search of pupils, I suppose?"

"Yes. He was rather disappointed to learn that I had none for him. He asked about Rosie and Walter, but I was unable to tell him positively whether they would, or would not, be sent to him. I gave him little encouragement, perhaps I should say none at all, to expect them."

"No. I am nearly certain they will not be willing to go to him, and that mamma will not care to send them. Indeed she more than hinted that she would be delighted to commit them to your care should you show yourself willing to undertake the task of instructing them. Are you willing?"

"I am hardly prepared to answer that question, my dear," he replied thoughtfully. "They may not be willing to submit to the authority of a brother-in-law."

"I am almost sure you would have no trouble in governing them," returned Violet.

"I don't believe you would have any at all, papa," remarked Lulu, who was leaning on the arm of his chair and listening with much interest to the conversation. "Neither of them is half so—so willful and quick-tempered as I am."

The captain smiled at that, put an arm about her, and drew her closer to him. "But they don't belong to me as you do," he said, touching his lips to her cheek. "You are my very own little daughter."

"Yes, indeed, and I am so glad to be," she returned, putting her arm round his neck and gazing into his eyes, her own shining with filial love.

The younger ones were already in bed, even Gracie having felt too fatigued with the duties and pleasures of the day to wait for evening prayers.

"Yes, I think you may esteem yourself a fortunate child in that respect, Lu," said Violet. "I really believe it is the next best thing to being his wife," she added with a pleasant little laugh.

"I think it's the very best thing, Mamma Vi," returned Lulu.

"Well, to get back to the original topic of our discourse, Levis—or at least to the question whether you are willing to undertake the tutelage of my young sister and brother," Violet went on. "I feel certain they would give you no trouble in governing them and also that your talent for teaching is such that they could not fail to greatly improve under your instruction."

"But might not your grandpa feel that I was interfering with him?" queried the captain.

"Oh, no, indeed! Grandpa feels that he is growing older now, and that he has done enough of that kind of work. And you would be glad to please mamma, my dear?"

"Most certainly. I could refuse her nothing—the poor, dear woman!"

"Then we may consider it settled? Oh, thank you, my dear."

"Well, yes. I suppose so. Are you willing to share your teacher with Rosie and Walter, daughter mine?" he asked, softly stroking Lulu's hair.

"My teacher, but not my father, you dear papa," returned Lulu, patting his cheek then holding up her face for a kiss, which he gave heartily and repeated more than once.

"What do you think, Mamma Vi, of your own husband having an amanuensis?" he continued, affectionately squeezing Lulu's hand, which he had taken in his. "My correspondence was disposed of today with the most unusual and unexpected ease. I would read a letter, tell my amanuensis the reply I wished to make, and she would write it off on the typewriter while I examined the next epistle, asking few directions and making scarcely any mistakes."

"Lulu did it?" Violet exclaimed in surprise. "Why, Lu, I am both astonished and delighted!"

"Thank you, Mamma Vi, and I am very glad that I can help my dear, kind father, who does so much for me," Lulu answered, putting her arm round his neck and laying her cheek to his. "Oh, I couldn't possibly do half enough for him! But I hope I may be a great deal of use to him some of these days."

"You are that already, dear child," he said. "So useful and so dear that your father would not know how to do without you."

"How good of you to say that, papa, but I am sure it would be ten times worse for me to be without you," she returned. "Oh, I'm glad I'm not a boy, to have to go away from you."

"I am glad, too," he responded. "I am glad that my children are neither all boys nor all girls. It is quite delightful, I think, to have some of each."

"Yes, sir. I think it's delightful to have both some brothers and some sisters when they are as good a sort as mine are, though I've seen some I'd be sorry to have."

"As I have seen some children that I should be sorry, I think, to call my own. Yet if they were mine I would probably love them dearly and perhaps not see their faults, or rather love them in spite of their naughtiness."

"Just as you do me, papa," she said a little sadly. "Haven't you always loved me, though I have sometimes been very, very naughty, indeed?"

"Yes, always," he said, holding her close, as something very dear and precious. "And I believe my little girl has always loved me even when I have been quite severe in the punishment of her faults."

"Yes, oh, yes, indeed, papa! Because I have always felt that I deserved it—often a much more severe punishment than you inflicted. And that you didn't do it because you liked to, but because you wanted to make me good."

"And happy," he added. "I think you are never happy when disobedient, willful, or ill-tempered."

"No, indeed, papa! And I'm thankful to you that you have never indulged me in those things."

"And I think, with Lu, that you are one of the best fathers, Levis," remarked Violet.

"It is certainly very pleasant to be so highly esteemed by one's wife and daughter, whether deserving of it or not," he said with a pleased little laugh. "Yet, I am not at all sure that such flattery is quite good for me."

"I don't believe any amount of praise could ever hurt you, papa," Lulu said with a look into his eyes of ardent love and reverence. "You do seem to me to be just perfect, never doing or saying anything wrong at all."

"I think it must be my little girl's great love for her father that makes her so blind to his faults and failings," he replied in low, tender tones.

"A blindness certainly shared by your wife," remarked Violet lightly. "We have been married five years, and I have yet to hear the first unkind word from my husband's lips."

"He would be an exceedingly unreasonable man who could find fault with such a wife as mine," was his smiling rejoinder.

"But to change the subject, I suppose we may look for the rest of our party about the last of next week, can't we?"

"Yes, I think so."

"I shall be ever so glad to see them—especially dear Grandma Elsie and Rosie and Walter. But, oh, I wish the Fairview folks were coming, especially Eva," remarked Lulu, ending with a sigh of regret.

"Ah, well, daughter, perhaps Evelyn may be here before the winter is over," the captain said, exchanging a slightly amused glance with Violet.

"Oh, I hope so!" exclaimed Lulu. "Of course, one can't expect to have everything one wants."

"No, certainly not," her father said. "It would be by no means good for us if we could."

"Not for me, I know. But, oh, I have a great many blessings—health and strength and such a dear kind father to love me, provide for me, teach me, and train me up in the way I should go," she concluded with a smiling look up into his eyes.

"That is what I am trying to do, at all events," he returned, holding her close. "Though I sometimes fear I may not always have taken the wisest way."

"Is it because you have succeeded so poorly that you fear so, papa?" she asked. "If so, don't be troubled about it, because I don't believe it's from any mistake of yours, but only that I'm so very naughty and unmanageable."

"Really, Lu, I think your father has succeeded fairly well at the business," laughed Violet. "I doubt if anybody else would have done better."

"Or half so well," said Lulu. "And I am fully resolved to try to do credit to his training."

"Did you have a letter from Max today, Levis?" remarked Violet inquiringly. "Dear fellow, I hope he was quite well at the time of writing?"

"Yes, and apparently in excellent spirits. He seems to be doing well in his studies and content with things as they are, though evidently feeling that he would greatly enjoy being here with the rest of us."

"Yes, poor, dear fellow! I wish he could make one of our party—especially at Christmas time."

"So do I," said his father. "We must make it up to him with as full an account as possible of the Christmas doings here."

"I wonder what they will be," said Lulu.

"We will have to consider and decide that and other questions—to some extent, at least—after mamma comes," replied Violet.

"And now we must go in and have prayers, for it is near bedtime for my eldest daughter," remarked the captain, rising and taking Lulu's hand in his.

The days flew by on swift wings, even to Lulu and Gracie, so filled were they with duties and pleasures, and at length the time had come when Grandma Elsie and the others were expected by the evening boat.

Their arrival was anticipated with great delight by everyone on the estate, and all possible preparations had been made for their comfort and to show how gladly welcome they were. Everything indoors and out was in beautiful order, a feast of fat things ready in the kitchen, the families from the parsonage and Magnolia Hall were present by invitation, and as the hour drew near when the boat might be expected, all gathered at the wharf and eagerly watched for its appearance.

At length their patience was rewarded. The little steamer appeared in sight far down the bayou, came puffing along past the orange orchard, and rounded to at the landing.

In another moment the travelers were on shore—Mr. and Mrs. Dinsmore, Grandma Elsie, Rosie and Walter, and—could Lulu believe her eyes—yes, there was Evelyn! It could be no one else, and with a cry of joy, the two little girls ran into each other's arms.

"Oh, Eva, Eva, I'm so glad! I hadn't the least idea that you were coming, too!" cried Lulu, fairly wild with delight.

"Ah, papa, you must have known and kept it a secret from me to give me such a glad surprise," she exclaimed, as she caught sight of his face and noted the pleased smile with which he was regarding her.

"Yes, daughter, I knew and planned with Mamma Vi and the others to give you this pleasant surprise," he said, bending down to bestow a paternal kiss upon the gentle, fatherless girl who had won so large a place in the heart of his and his own dear child.

"And we were all very glad to have Eva along," Rosie said. "And, oh, Lu, I'm looking for very good times this coming winter here in our lovely Viamede, and with your father here I know it will be pleasanter than ever for you — pleasanter for all of us. Brother Levis, I hear that I am to be your pupil instead of Professor Manton's — a change which I haven't a doubt I shall enjoy extremely."

"Ah, don't be too sure of that, little sister," he returned laughingly, giving a welcoming embrace to her also. "I am a very strict disciplinarian, as Lulu here can testify," laying a hand affectionately on his daughter's shoulder.

"Yes, Rosie, papa is strict, but if one does as he orders, he's kind as can be. Maybe he wouldn't be quite so stern and strict with other folks' children as he is with me — his very own, you know."

But a reply from Rosie was prevented by Violet catching her in her arms, saying, "You dear child, how glad I am to have you here at last! We have all been looking forward to your coming as well as to that of dear, darling mamma, grandpa, and the others."

At the same time Grandma Elsie was embracing Lulu most affectionately, saying how well she looked and hoping that she and Gracie, as well as the older people, had been enjoying Viamede.

"Indeed we have, dear Grandma Elsie," replied Lulu. "Oh, it was so good and kind of you to invite us all to spend the winter in this loveliest of all the lovely places!"

"Good to myself, dear child, quite as much as to you, for I love to have you all about me."

"And I hope you are better? A great deal better?" returned Lulu with a genuinely concerned look into the sweet face.

"Very much better, thank you, dear child. Almost my old self again," was the sweet-toned reply.

Some few moments more were spent in the exchange of glad, affectionate greetings and inquiries after each other's health and welfare, then all took their way to the house. Even Grandma Elsie claimed that her strength was quite equal to so short a walk, the journey on the boat having been more restful than fatiguing. Yet it was evident to all that she was far from strong, and they joined Mr. Dinsmore in an urgent entreaty that she would retire at an early hour to her own room and bed. She did as she was bidden, her daughters accompanying her to see that nothing was lacking that could in any way add to her comfort.

CHAPTER
NINETEENTH

A BRIGHT, BEAUTIFUL day succeeded the one on which the Ion family had arrived at Viamede. The younger members of their party awoke early, and the sun was hardly more than an hour high when Evelyn and Rosie passed down the broad stairway into the lower hall, moving with cautious tread lest they might disturb the still sleeping older members of the household.

On approaching the veranda they were surprised to see the captain and Lulu already taking their morning promenade along the bank of the bayou.

"Ah, I see there is no getting ahead of Brother Levis," laughed Rosie. "Let us run down there and join them, Eva."

"With all my heart," returned Evelyn merrily, and away they went, racing down the broad, graveled walk in merry, girlish fashion.

"Good morning, little ladies, I see that you are early birds as well as Lulu and myself," the captain said with his genial smile, as they drew near.

"Yes, sir," returned Rosie, catching hold of Lulu and giving her a hearty embrace. "On such a morning as this, and in such a lovely place, bed has no attractions to compare with those of out of doors."

"That's exactly what papa and I think," said Lulu. "Oh girls, I'm so glad you have come to share this lovely, lovely place with us. Eva, I haven't yet got over the glad surprise of your coming. I was just saying to papa how kind it was of Grandma Elsie and the rest of them to prepare such an unexpected pleasure for me. Wasn't it good of them?"

"Yes, indeed, good to us both!" Evelyn said, squeezing affectionately the hand Lulu had slipped into hers.

"Captain," looking up smilingly into his face, "are you intending to be so very, very kind as to take me for one of your pupils?"

"Most assuredly, my dear, if you wish it," he replied without hesitation.

"Oh, thank you, sir! Thank you very much indeed, and I promise to give you as little trouble as I possibly can."

"I shall consider it no trouble at all, my dear child," he returned, giving her a fatherly smile. "Indeed, I think the favor will be on your side, as doubtless Lulu will improve all the faster for your companionship in her studies. Rosie, being older than either of you, will, I fear, have to be quite alone in most of hers."

"Yes, Brother Levis, and as I am to be such a lonely, forlorn creature you ought to be extremely good to me," remarked Rosie demurely. "I hope you will remember that and try to have unlimited patience with your younger sister."

"Ah! My little sister would better not try the patience of her big brother too far," returned the captain with a twinkle of fun in his eye.

"I dare say, but he needn't think he can make me much afraid of him, big as he is," laughed Rosie.

"Perhaps, though, it might yet turn out to the advantage of Professor Manton, should my youngest sister prove quite beyond the management of her biggest and oldest brother," remarked the captain with assumed gravity.

"There!" exclaimed Rosie. "That's the worst threat you could possibly have made. I think I'll try to be at least passably good and obedient in the school-room. You needn't look for it in any other place, Captain Raymond," making him a deep curtsey, then dancing merrily away.

"Don't you envy that it is only in the schoolroom she must be obedient to me, whom you have to obey all the time?" asked the captain laughingly of Lulu, noticing that she was watching Rosie with a hurt, indignant look on her very expressive features.

"No, indeed, papa! I'm only too glad that I belong to you everywhere and all the time," she answered, lifting to his face eyes full of filial respect and ardent affection.

"So am I," he returned, pressing tenderly the hand she had again slipped into his. "But you must not be vexed with Rosie. Could you not see that all she said just now was in sportive jest?"

"I'm glad if she didn't mean it, papa. But I also don't like such things said to my dear, honored father — even in jest."

"But you must excuse Rosie, Lu, dear," said Evelyn. "It was indeed all in jest, for I know that she feels the very highest respect for your father — her biggest brother — as we all do."

Lulu's brow cleared. "Well, then, I won't mind it, papa, if you don't," she said.

"I certainly do not, daughter," he remarked in his usual pleasant way. "Rosie and I are the best of friends, and I think will continue to be such."

It was a merry, light-hearted party that met at the Viamede breakfast table that morning. Even their loved invalid, Grandma Elsie, was looking wonderfully bright and well. Yet, as she laughingly averred, everybody seemed determined to consider her as ill and unable to make any exertion.

"I shall have to let you continue to take the role of mistress of the establishment, Vi," she said with a pleasant smile, as, resigning to her daughter her accustomed seat at the head of the table, she took possession of one at the side.

"Not that I am of so humble a spirit as to consider myself unfitted for the duties and responsibilities of the position, but only because older and wiser people do."

"I really think Vi makes as good a substitute as could well be found, mother," remarked the captain with a proudly affectionate glance at his lovely young wife.

"In which I entirely agree with you, sir," said Mr. Dinsmore.

The meal was partaken of with appetite and enlivened by cheery talk—a good deal of it in regard to pleasures and amusements attainable in that locality. There was riding, driving, boating, fishing—to say nothing of the pleasant rambles that could be taken on or beyond the estate.

There were no lack of carriages for driving, or horses to draw them, or for those to ride who might prefer that mode of locomotion.

The final decision was in favor of a drive for Mrs. Dinsmore, Violet, her little ones, and Gracie, accompanied by the rest of the party on horseback.

Breakfast and family prayers over, the young girls hastened to their rooms to prepare for their little excursion, all seemingly in the merriest spirits at the pleasing prospect. There was none more so than merry, excitable Lulu.

She and Gracie were ready a little sooner than either of the other girls, and they went down to the veranda to wait there for the rest.

As they did so a servant passed them with the bag containing the morning mail, which he had just brought from the nearest post office.

He carried it to the library, where Mr. Dinsmore and the captain were seated, awaiting the appearance of the ladies, carriages, and horses.

As if struck by a sudden thought, Lulu ran after him. She saw her father take the bag, open it, hand several letters to Mr. Dinsmore, select several others and give them to the servant with directions to carry them up to the ladies, then lay a pretty large pile on the table, take up one, and open it.

"There, those are papa's own," she said to herself. "What a number he has! They all have to be answered, too. I don't believe he'll take time to ride this morning; he's always so prompt about replying to a letter. Oh, dear, I don't want to go without him, and I just wish they hadn't come till tomorrow." She walked slowly out to the veranda again.

Neither Rosie nor Evelyn had yet made their appearance, and Gracie was romping about with little Elsie and Ned.

Just then a servant man came around the stables, leading the ponies the three little girls were to ride, and at sight of them Lulu seemed to take a very sudden resolution.

"Oh, Solon," she said, hurrying toward the man, "you can put my pony back into the stable. I'm not going to ride this morning. I've changed my mind, and if anybody asks about me, you can tell them so." And with that she ran away around the house and seated herself on the back veranda, where she had been when Professor Manton made his call upon the captain.

Presently she heard the ladies and young girls come down the stairs, her father and Mr. Dinsmore come out of the library and assist the older ones into the carriage, the younger to mount their ponies. Then her father's voice asking, "Where is Lulu?" and the servant's reply, "Miss Lu, she tole me, sah, to tell you she doan want fo' to ride dis heah mornin', sah." Then her father's surprised, "She did, Solon?" Why, that's a sudden change on her part. I thought she was quite delighted at the prospect of going.

"Violet, my dear, I find I have so many letters calling for a reply this morning, that I, too, must remain at home."

Some exclamations of surprise and regret from the others followed. The sound of hoofs and wheels told that the party had set out on their little excursion, and the captain's step was heard in the hall as he returned to the library.

But a thought seemed to strike him as he reached the door, and he paused, calling aloud, "Lulu!"

She ran to him at once, answering his call, "Here I am, papa."

"Why, daughter, what is the meaning of this?" he asked. "Why did you not go with the others?"

"Because I preferred to stay at home with my dear father, and I hope he isn't displeased with me for it!" she replied, looking up coaxingly, smilingly, into his face.

"Displeased with you, dear child? I am only too glad to have you by my side, except that I feel sorry on your account that you should miss the pleasant, healthful trip along with the others," he said, bestowing upon her a fond caress.

"But how did you know I was going to stay at home?" he asked, as he led her in and sat down, drawing her to a seat upon his knee.

"Because I'm enough of a Yankee to be good at guessing, I suppose, papa," she answered with a merry laugh, putting her arm round his neck and gazing into his eyes with her own full of ardent filial love. "I saw that big pile of letters," pointing to them as they lay on the table. "And I thought, 'Now, if I stay at home with papa, maybe he will let me help him as I did the other day.' So now as I have stayed, won't you be so very good as to let me, you dear, dearest papa?"

"I shall be very glad of both your company and your help, darling, though I am sorry to have you miss your ride in order to give them to me."

"But you needn't be sorry, papa, because I'm ever so glad. I was almost afraid you might be displeased with me for taking the liberty of staying at home without consulting you, but I don't believe you are a bit," stroking his face with her soft, white hand, then kissing him with warmth of affection.

"I am so much displeased, that as a punishment you will have to write several letters on your machine at my dictation," he replied with playful look and tone. "We will set to work at once," he added, putting her off his knee, taking the cover from her typewriter, placing a chair before it for her to sit upon, and then laying a pile of paper and envelopes within easy reach of her hand.

"Ah, papa, I don't care how often you punish me in this way!" she exclaimed with a merry laugh, as she took her seat.

"Tut! Tut! Don't talk as if my punishment were nothing," he replied in pretend displeasure. "You may get more of this kind some of these days than you will like."

"Not while it's a help to my dear father," she returned, smiling up at him.

"You find that a pleasure, do you?" he asked with tender look and tone, laying a hand caressingly on her head and gazing fondly down into her eyes.

"Yes, indeed, sir! Oh, papa, I just long to be a real help and comfort and blessing to you. I do hope that some day I may be."

"My own dear little daughter, you are already all three to me," he said with emotion. "Truly, I think no man ever had a more lovable child, or a more grateful and appreciative one."

Those words sent a thrill of exquisite delight to Lulu's heart. "Dear papa, you are so kind to tell me that!" she exclaimed. "Oh, I do want always to be all that to you!"

"And it is certainly my ardent desire to be the best of fathers to my dear eldest daughter and all my children," he responded.

"Now, let us set to work on this correspondence."

For the next hour and more father and daughter were very busy at their letter writing. Then, every letter having been replied to, the captain went out to a distant part of the plantation to see how work was progressing, taking Lulu along with him.

Their way led them through the orange orchard, and both father and daughter found it quite a delightful walk.

They reached home again just in time to receive the others of their party upon their return from their little excursion, and presently after, all sat down to dinner.

Upon leaving the dinner table the little girls repaired to the veranda.

"I'm decidedly offended with you, Lu," said Rosie in jesting tone.

"What for?" asked Lulu.

"For forsaking us as you did this morning, and now the least reparation you can make is to confess why you did so. Do you not agree with me, Eva?"

"Yes," replied Evelyn. "I think she ought to do so, as the only amends she can make. So, Miss Raymond, let us hear your excuse at once—if you have any."

"Well, then, I suppose I must," said Lulu. "Please understand that I would have enjoyed going with you very much indeed, but I saw that papa had a good many letters to answer. I wanted to help him a great deal more that I did to take a ride.

"He lets me write some on the typewriter—those you see, that don't require a very particular answer. He says it shortens his work very much. And," she added with a sigh, "I have given my dear father so much trouble in past days by my bad temper and willfulness, that I feel I can never do enough to make up to him for it."

"Dear Lu, I just love you for acting so," said Evelyn, softly, giving Lulu's hand an affectionate squeeze as she spoke. "And I am sure your father must as well."

"Yes, he does love me dearly, and you can't think how happy that makes me," returned Lulu, glad tears shining in her eyes.

"I don't know about that, but I think we can," said Rosie, a slight tremble in her voice. She had not forgotten altogether the dear father who had hugged and kissed her in her babyhood, but who had so long since passed away to the better land.

But just at that moment Violet drew near with a light, quick step.

"The boat is at the landing, little girls," she said. "And we older folks want to be off. Please put on your hats—coats, too. Or you may carry some kind of wrap, for the captain says it may be quite cool on the water before we return."

"A summons we're delighted to receive," returned Rosie, springing to her feet and hurrying toward the hall door, the others following, all of them in a merry good humor.

No one was missing from that boating excursion, and on their return, a little before teatime, all spoke of having a most enjoyable afternoon.

CHAPTER TWENTIETH

AFTER TEA, WHEN all were together upon the front veranda, Grandma Elsie in a reclining chair, the others grouped about her, the talk turned upon approaching Christmas and how it should be celebrated — what gifts prepared for friends and servants.

Various plans were suggested; various gifts were spoken of; but nothing was firmly settled.

The little girls took a deep interest in the subject, and when they separated for the night each one's thoughts were full of it. Lulu's were more full perhaps than those of any other, not of what she might receive, but what she would like to give.

"Papa," she said, when he came into her room to bid her goodnight, "I do so want to make some pretty things to give at Christmas time. Please, won't you let me?" Her look and tone were very coaxing.

"My dear little daughter," he replied, taking possession of an easy chair and drawing her to a seat upon his knee, "it would give me much pleasure to indulge you in this, but you have lost a good deal of time from your studies of late. I know very well that to allow you to engage in the manufacture of Christmas gifts would have the effect of taking your mind off your lessons in a way to prevent you from making much, if any, progress with them."

"Then you won't let me, papa?"

"No, child. If you choose you may use your own pocket money and some more that I will give you to buy what you please, so long as it will not make any work for you. Your studies must be faithfully attended to, and the greater part of your remaining time I wish you to spend in outdoor amusements which will, I hope, both give you much pleasure and keep you in vigorous health.

"I could not bear to see my dear, eldest daughter growing pale and thin, or failing to improve her mind and talents so that she may in due time become a noble, useful woman, capable of doing with her might whatever work her heavenly Father may be pleased to give her."

A woefully ill-used, discontented look had come over Lulu's expressive countenance as her father began what he had to say, but before he had finished it was replaced by a sweeter one of contentment with his decision and confiding filial love.

"Papa, dear, I did at first very much want you to say yes to my petition, but now I see that you know best and am quite content to do as you have said you want me to," she returned, putting her arm about his neck and laying her cheek to his in her accustomed fashion when her heart was swelling with daughterly affection.

"My dear child, your ready acquiescence in your father's decision makes you dearer than ever to him, if that is possible," he said, holding her close with many a fond caress.

Meanwhile Rosie and Evelyn, each occupying adjoining rooms, were chatting merrily of what they should make for one and another of those they loved and admired.

Suddenly Evelyn paused, a very thoughtful look overspreading her expressive face.

"Well, what is it?" asked Rosie in a bantering tone. Evelyn answered, "I was just thinking that all this, should we undertake it, will be apt to take our minds from our lessons, which are certainly of far greater importance."

"And that Captain Raymond may veto it upon that account?" asked Rosie with a twinkle of fun in her eye.

"Possibly he may, and if he does, I, for one, shall certainly obey him," replied Evelyn, speaking in a sober, earnest way that said plainly she was far from being in jest.

"Well, I make no rash promises," laughed Rosie. "And I'm not very much afraid of that brother-in-law of mine, stern as he can look when it suits him."

"But you will want to please your dear mother?" returned Evelyn in a tone somewhere between assertion and inquiry.

"Yes," replied Rosie, sobering down at once. "I could refuse nothing to dear mamma. I would do anything and everything in my power to add to her happiness. Oh, how glad and thankful I am that she has been spared to us!"

"I, too," said Evelyn. "I think I could hardly love her better if she were really my very near relative."

A moment of silence followed, presently broken by Rosie. "Well, I suppose," she said with a return to her jesting tone, "it may be our wisest plan to consult his lordship—Captain Raymond—in regard to the matter just now under discussion. The subject as to whether we—his prospective pupils—may or may not engage in the work of preparing Christmas gifts for other folk."

"I, at least, certainly intend to do so," replied Evelyn. "Obedience to his wishes — to say nothing of orders — it strikes me, will be the very least we can do in return for his great kindness in taking the trouble to instruct us."

"There you are right!" said Rosie. "I hadn't thought of that before. It is very good of him and I shall try to show him that I am one of the best and most tractable of pupils."

"Suppose we join him and Lu tomorrow in their morning walk, as we did today. Then and there take the opportunity to discuss this momentous question," suggested Evelyn laughingly.

"I am strongly in favor of so doing, provided I wake in season," returned Rosie, and with that they separated for the night.

They carried out their plan, had a pleasant little morning ramble and chat with the captain and Lulu, and finding that such was his wish, promised to do but little in the way of making Christmas gifts in order that their time and attention might be more fully occupied with their studies, which they were all to take up again on the following Monday.

"This being Friday, we have only today and tomorrow for play. It looks like rain, too," sighed Rosie disconsolately, glancing up at the sky as she spoke. "So we are not likely to have much of the out-of-door sort of sport."

"Ah, well, little sister, we must not grumble about the rain, for it is needed. And there are the verandas for you young folks to sport upon," returned the captain pleasantly.

"Besides your big brother is not intending to be so hard upon you as to allow no diversion after lessons are resumed. I hope you will all have many an hour for romping, riding, driving, boating, and walking among other things."

"Pleasant chats, too, and interesting books to read; music and games besides," remarked Evelyn. "Oh, we are not likely to suffer from lack of diversion when we have been good and industrious enough to deserve it," she added with a smiling look at the captain.

"As I have little doubt that you will be always," he returned, smiling kindly upon her.

By the time breakfast and family worship were over, a gentle rain was falling, and instead of seeking out-of-door amusement, the whole family gathered upon the veranda at the front of the house.

Just then a pretty well-filled mailbag made its appearance, and presently everybody had one or more letter in hand.

Noticing that her father had several, Lulu presently drew near him and asked, "Mayn't I help you answer those, papa?"

"Thank you, dear child, " he returned, smiling fondly upon her. "You may if you wish, but I have plenty of time to do the work myself this morning. I would be sorry to deprive you of the pleasure you might be taking with your mates."

"I'll have time enough for that afterward, papa, and would very much rather do a little to help you — if it will be a help, instead of a trouble to you to have me use my machine in that way," she said with a look up into his eyes that showed plainly how anxious she was to have her offer accepted.

"Then you shall, indeed, my little darling," he returned. Taking her tiny hand into his larger one, he led her into the library, seated her before her typewriter, supplied paper and envelopes, and began dictating responses to his letters to her, as on the two former occasions.

"It grieves me to rob my dear little girl of any of her holiday time," he remarked, as the first letter was completed, laying his hand caressingly on her head. "Your father really does love to see you enjoying yourself."

"Yes, dear papa, I know that," she replied with a pleased, loving look up into his face. "But there is nothing I enjoy more than feeling that I can be of a little help and comfort to you."

"Well, it will not take us long to answer these letters — there are but few today — and perhaps you may enjoy your sports all the more afterward," he replied, handing her a fresh sheet of paper.

※ ※ ※ ※ ※

"This, from our dear Max, is the only one left now," he remarked presently. "And he, I know, would rather have his reply in his papa's own handwriting. Shall I read this to you, daughter?"

"I should like to hear it, papa!" was her eager response. "May I sit on your knee while I listen?"

"Indeed you may," he answered, drawing her to the coveted seat and putting his arm about her waist. "Maxie does write such good, interesting letters, and I'm so much obliged to you for reading this one to me, papa," she said when he had finished.

"You are very welcome, daughter. Now you may go back to your mates while I write my reply."

On the veranda, family letters had been read and discussed, meanwhile, and when Lulu rejoined the group, they were again talking of the approaching

Christmas and what gifts should be prepared for relatives, near and dear friends, and servants.

Grandma Elsie, seated in their midst, was looking quite herself — very bright, beautiful, and sweet.

"With the housekeeping given in charge to Vi," she was saying, as Lulu drew near, "I shall have an abundance of spare time and hope to prepare many gifts for—"

"No," interrupted her father. "You are to do nothing of the kind. You must devote yourself to the business of gaining strength as fast as possible."

She laughed pleasantly at that, saying, "Papa, my vacation has been a long one already, for I have really done nothing worth speaking of since we returned home from the North."

"And what of that, daughter?" he responded. "You have never been an idler, but it seems to be time now for you to begin. Let your vacation go on till next spring. That is my prescription for you."

"Ah, ha, mamma!" laughed Rosie. "The captain forbids Christmas gift making for us younger ones, and I'm mighty glad grandpa forbids it to you. 'Misery loves company,' you know."

"I hope my Rosie may never be called upon to share any worse misery," was the smiling rejoinder. "I also trust that she will show herself as obedient to the captain as I intend to be to her kind, loving grandpa—so careful of his daughter," with a fond look up into her father's face.

"As he may well be, for she is a treasure worth guarding," he said, returning her look of love. "Rosie, when does the captain propose beginning his labor as tutor?"

"Monday morning, grandpa, so we want to crowd all the fun we can into today and tomorrow."

"Ah, we must select a schoolroom at once and furnish it with whatever may be necessary!" exclaimed Violet.

"Yes," her mother said. "The room used for that purpose when you were a very little girl will answer nicely. Its desks were sent to the attic when no longer needed. You might order them brought down today, the room swept and dusted, and whatever else done that is necessary or desirable, so that it will be quite ready for occupation on Monday."

"Thank you, mamma. I will have it attended to at once," Violet replied and hastened away, as Rosie ran after her with a, "Come, girls, let us go and see the room and find out whether it has a closet for the captain to shut us up in when we misbehave."

"I don't believe he'll use it if it has," laughed Lulu, rather enjoying Rosie's fun with her brother-in-law. "He has never punished any of us—his own children—in that way."

"Still there is no knowing but he may take a new departure, now, when he's going to have so distinguished a pupil as myself," pursued Rosie, dancing down the hall with the others close in her rear.

They followed Violet to the room Grandma Elsie had spoken of and found it large and airy with windows down to the floor opening out upon the veranda on that side of the house. The walls were prettily papered and adorned with good pictures, handsomely framed. The floor was covered with fine matting, furniture handsome, a pretty clock and vases on the mantel. On one side of that was a door to which Rosie flew and, throwing it wide open, brought to view a large closet.

"There!" she exclaimed. "Didn't I tell you, girls and Walter?" for he was in the company by that time. "Here's the place of incarceration for those who shall dare to disobey Captain Raymond. I for one shall certainly try to behave my prettiest, for I wouldn't like to be shut up in the dark."

"Well, it certainly appears to me, sister that you are more likely to come to it than any of the rest of us," observed Walter quietly, as he turned on his heel and walked away.

"Did you ever hear the like?" cried Rosie, opening her eyes wide in pretend astonishment.

"What's all this?" asked a familiar voice at the door. Turning at the sound, they saw Captain Raymond standing there, looking very grave and slightly reproving, but with a perceptible twinkle of fun in his eyes.

"We were just looking at the closet you are going to use for the incarceration of the naughty ones, for this is to be your schoolroom, you see, sir," returned Rosie demurely.

"And you expect to enjoy a sojourn there?" he queried, coming forward and himself taking a survey of the interior. "It strikes me it would suit better as a receptacle for school books and the like."

"So it would," she said with a sigh of pretend relief. "We, your pupils that are to be, will venture to hope that you will see best to devote it to that use."

"A hope in which you will not be disappointed, I trust," he replied in a kindly tone, laying a hand lightly on her shoulder.

"There, girls!" she exclaimed. "You may thank me for extracting such a promise beforehand. I do really believe his honor intends to treat us well if we are reasonably well behaved."

"And the rest of us are quite sure of it," added Evelyn with a bright look up into the captain's face.

"Thank you for your confidence, my dear," he returned. "I have little doubt that we will have pleasant times together in this very pleasant room."

A little more time was spent in examining the room and commenting upon its beauties and conveniences. Then they went back to the veranda to find that the sun had just begun to peep through the clouds.

So carriages were ordered, and all took a drive through the beautiful woods.

The afternoon was spent in boating and fishing, the evening on the veranda, where they were joined by their relatives from both Magnolia Hall and the parsonage as well.

The manner in which they would spend the approaching Christmas and New Year's Day was the principal subject of conversation, and the young folks were particularly interested in listening to the plans made or suggested. They were well satisfied with the proposed arrangement that the cousins should spend the first at Viamede, all gather at Magnolia Hall for their New Year's dinner and pass the evening of that day at the parsonage.

❧ ❧ ❧ ❧ ❧

Lulu had a talk with her father at bedtime that made her very happy and entirely contented with his prohibition of the making of gifts.

He told her that she and Gracie might each make out a list of the articles they would like to buy to present to others, and that some one, probably Mr. Embury—Cousin Molly's husband—who was intending to pay a visit of a few days to New

Orleans, would kindly make the purchases for them while he was there.

"Oh, that will do nicely, papa!" she exclaimed delightedly. "And Gracie and I might make out our lists tomorrow with a little help from our dear father," smiling up into his eyes.

"Yes, dear child, I will gladly give you both all the assistance in my power," he replied, softly smoothing her hair, for she was—as usual at such times—sitting upon his knee. "And not with advice only," he continued, "but also by adding something to your means for carrying out your wishes."

"Oh, you dear papa, you are just the kindest father that ever was made!" she cried in an ecstasy of delight, hugging him with all her strength.

"Ah, but if you choke me to death," he said laughingly, "I can do nothing to help you."

"Oh, papa, please excuse me!" she exclaimed, relaxing her hold. "Did I hurt you? Oh, I am very, very sorry!"

"Not much. I could stand it very well," he returned, giving her a hug and a kiss. "But now I must leave you to go to bed and to sleep."

CHAPTER
TWENTY-FIRST

THERE WAS A DECIDED downpour of rain the next morning, but no one minded that very much, as the necessity for staying within doors gave time and opportunity for further arrangements in regard to Christmas and the gifts to be presented.

The captain kindly devoted an hour or more to helping his little girls to decide upon theirs and make out a list. Mr. Embury, Molly, and Isadore, who were intending to accompany him to the city, having kindly offered to make any purchases desired by the Viamede relatives.

At the same time the others, older and younger, were similarly engaged, and there were many little private chats as they gathered in two's and three's here and there about the veranda or in the rooms.

In the afternoon Violet invited the whole party to inspect the schoolroom, where some of the servants had been busy under her direction all the morning, giving it a thorough cleaning, draping the windows with fresh lace curtains looped back with blue ribbons, and placing a desk for each expected pupil, along with a neat table for the teacher.

Every one pronounced it a model schoolroom, some of the older people adding that it made them almost wish themselves young enough to again be busy with lessons and recitations.

"Where's your ferule, Brother Levis?" asked Rosie facetiously after a close scrutiny of the table, not omitting its drawer.

"I think you have not made a very thorough examination of the closet yet," came his rather noncommittal reply.

"Oh, that's where you keep it? I say girls —" in a loud whisper, perfectly audible to everyone in the room, "let's carry it off before he has a chance to use it."

"Hardly worth while, since it would be of no difficulty to replace it," remarked the captain with assumed gravity and sternness.

"Ah, then I suppose one may as well be resigned to circumstances," sighed Rosie, following the others from the room.

"Papa, can I help you?" asked Lulu, seeing him seat himself at the table in the library, take out writing materials from its drawer, and dip a pen into the ink.

"No, thank you, daughter," he replied. "I am going to write to Max."

"Please tell him we are all ever so sorry he can't be here to spend Christmas and New Year's with all of us."

"I will."

"And he can't have the pleasure of giving any gifts, I suppose, as they allow him so little pocket money of his own!"

"Dear boy! He shall not miss that pleasure entirely," said the captain. "I am going now to write him that I will set apart a certain sum for his use in the purchase of gifts for others. That is, he may tell me what he would like to give, and I will see that the articles are bought and distributed as he wishes."

"Oh, what a nice plan, papa! I am sure Maxie will be very glad."

"Yes, I do it with the hope of giving pleasure to my dear boy. And besides that I shall tell him that he may again choose some benevolent object to which I will give, in his name, a thousand dollars. You, too, and Gracie shall have the same privilege."

"Just as we all had last year. Oh, papa, it is so good and kind of you!"

"That is the opinion of my partial little daughter," he returned with a smile. "But, daughter, as I have often told you, the money is the Lord's, and I am only His steward."

"Yes, sir," she said and walked thoughtfully away.

By the middle of the afternoon the rain seemed to be over, and a row on the bayou was enjoyed by most of the party—all who cared to go.

Music and conversation made the evening pass quickly and pleasantly, and all retired to their rooms at an early hour that they might arise refreshed for the duties and privileges of the Lord's day.

It was spent, as former ones had been, attending church and the pastor's Bible class in the morning and holding a similar service on the lawn at Viamede in the afternoon.

In addressing that little congregation on the grounds the captain tried very hard to make the way of salvation very clear and plain.

"It is just to come to Jesus as you are," he said. "Not waiting to make yourself better, for you never can. He alone can do that work; it is His blood that cleanses from all sin; his righteousness that is perfect, and therefore acceptable to God; while our righteousnesses are as filthy rags, stained and defiled with sin.

"Concerning Him—the only begotten Son of God—the Bible tells us, 'He is able to save them unto the uttermost that come unto God by him.'

"'The blood of Jesus Christ His Son cleanseth us from all sin.'

"And He says, 'Him that cometh to me I will in no wise cast out.'

"'This is the will of Him that sent Me, that every one who seeth the Son, and believeth on Him, may have everlasting life; and I will raise Him up at the last day.'

"Just go to Jesus each one of you, give yourself to Him and believe His word—that He will not cast you out; he will receive you and make you His own; giving you His spirit, changing you from the poor sinner you are, by nature, into His image, His Likeness."

At the conclusion of that service Lulu and Gracie recited their Bible verses and catechism to their father.

The evening was spent in conversation and music suited to the sacredness of the day, and all retired to their rest.

Nine o'clock the next morning found the girls and Walter seated in the schoolroom. Lulu and Gracie busied with their tasks, the others ready and waiting to have theirs appointed by the captain.

School that day was a decided success, and Rosie pretended that her fears of the new teacher were greatly allayed.

Between that and Christmastime everything moved along smoothly. Studies were well attended to, sports and pastimes greatly enjoyed.

The celebration of the holidays—Christmas and New Year's—also proved a great and grand success. There were many and beautiful gifts. A handsome brooch from the captain delighted each little girl, and there were so many other lovely gifts, they are too numerous to mention.

The distribution was on Christmas Eve. The next day there was a grand dinner at Viamede, all the relatives present, and everybody in merriest spirits.

The day was bright and beautiful, seeming but little like Christmas to those accustomed to frost and snow at that season.

New Year's Day was not less lovely, nor were its festivities less enjoyable, though the gifts were fewer then.

The holidays past, the young folks went back with zest to their studies, Rosie saying she was now convinced that Captain Raymond was an excellent teacher—not at all inclined to tyrannize over a well behaved pupil. He gravely thanked her for her complimentary expression of opinion.

"You are very welcome, sir," she said. "And you may depend upon a recommendation from me whenever it is wanted."

"Oh, Rosie, how ridiculous you are!" exclaimed Walter after his sister.

But Rosie was already out of the room, the other girls following. They went out on the lawn, ran about for a while, then settled themselves under a tree and began to crack and eat nuts.

Lulu was very fond of them, and presently she put one between her teeth and cracked it there.

"Oh, Lu!" exclaimed Gracie. "You forget that papa forbade you to crack nuts with your teeth, for fear you might break them."

"Well, I wanted to break the nut," returned Lulu, laughing, but then blushing because her conscience reproached her.

"I meant break your teeth," said Gracie. "I'm sure you wouldn't have done it—cracked the nut—if you hadn't forgotten that papa forbade you to do it."

"No, Gracie, I'm not so good as you think. I did not forget; I just did it because I wanted to," Lulu said with an evident effort, blushing again.

Then she sprang up and ran toward her father, who was seen at some little distance, coming from the orange orchard toward the house.

"I do believe she's going to tell on herself!" exclaimed Rosie in astonishment.

"Oh, dear, I wonder what papa will do to her!" exclaimed Gracie, just ready to burst into tears.

"It is very noble of her to go and confess at once, when he needn't have ever known anything about it," cried Eva admiringly.

They were all three watching Lulu and her father with intense interest, though too far away to hear anything that either one might say.

Lulu drew near him, hanging her head shamefully. "Papa," she said in a low, remorseful tone, "I have just been disobeying you."

"Ah! I am sorry, very sorry, to hear it, daughter," he returned a little sadly. Then, taking her hand, he led her away further from the house and seated her and himself on a bench beneath a group of trees that entirely hid them from view.

"Tell me the whole story, my child," he said, not unkindly, still keeping her hand in his.

"I cracked a nut with my teeth, papa," she replied with her eyes upon the ground and her cheek hot with blushes.

"You forgot that I had forbidden it?"

"No, papa, I haven't even that poor excuse. I remembered all the time that you had forbidden me, but just did it because I wanted to."

"Even though I have given you my reason for the prohibition — that you might risk serious damage to your teeth and probably suffer both pain and the loss of those useful members in consequence. It gives me great pain to find that my dear eldest daughter cares so little for her father's wishes or his commands."

At that Lulu burst into tears and sobs. "Oh, I hope you'll punish me well for it, papa!" she said. "I deserve it, and I think it would do me good."

"I must punish you for conduct so decidedly rebellious," he replied. "I will either forbid nuts for a week or refrain from giving you a caress for the same length of time. Which shall it be?"

"Oh, papa, I'd rather go without nuts for the rest of the winter than a whole week without a caress from you!" she exclaimed.

"Very well, then," he said, bending down and touching his lips to her cheek. "I forbid the nuts, and I think I can trust my daughter to obey me by not touching one till she has her father's permission to do so."

"I feel sure I will, papa," she said. "But if I should be so very bad as to disobey you again in this, I will come to you, confess it, and take my punishment without a word of objection."

"I have no doubt of it, daughter," he returned, taking her hand again and leading her back toward the house.

The other girls were awaiting with intense interest the reappearance of the captain and Lulu.

"Here they come!" exclaimed Rosie. "And I don't believe he has punished her. There has hardly been time, and though she looks very sober—he, too—she doesn't look at all frightened. Nor does he look angry, and he holds her hand in what strikes me as a very affectionate way."

"Yes," said Evelyn, "I think the captain is as good and kind a father as anyone could desire, and I'm sure Lulu's opinion of him is the same."

"Yes, indeed," asserted Gracie heartily, as she wiped the tears from her eyes. "There couldn't be a better, kinder father than ours. Lulu and I both think, but though he doesn't like to punish us, sometimes he feels that it's his duty to do it to make us good."

"I don't believe you get, or need, punishment very often, Gracie," remarked Rosie. "You are as good as gold—at least, so it seems to me."

"I'm not perfect, Rosie. Oh, no, indeed!" Gracie answered earnestly. "But papa almost never does anything more than talk in a grave, kind way to me about my faults."

By this time the captain and Lulu had drawn near the house. Letting go of her hand, he said, "You may go back to your mates now, daughter," he said in a kindly tone. "I have some matters to attend to, and if you have anything more to say to me, I will hear it at another time."

"Yes, sir," replied Lulu and went slowly toward the little group under the tree, while her father passed around to the other side of the house.

"He was not very much vexed with you, Lu, was he?" queried Rosie in a kindly inquiring tone, as Lulu joined them, looking grave and a trifle sad, while traces of tears could be discerned on her cheeks and about her eyes.

"Papa only seemed sorry that—that I could be so disobedient," faltered the little girl, tears starting to her eyes again. "But he always punishes disobedience, which is just what he ought to do, I am sure. He has forbidden me to eat any nuts for a week. I chose that rather than doing without a caress from him for the same length of time. So you see he was not very severe—not half so severe as I deserved that he should be."

The others agreed with her that it was but a light punishment, and then they began talking of something else.

Nuts were a part of the dessert that day, and Lulu, sitting near her father, asked in a low aside, "Papa, mayn't I pick out some kernels for you?"

"If you wish, daughter," he answered, and she performed the little service with evident pleasure.

"Thank you, dear child," he said with a loving look and smile as she handed them to him. Speaking of it to Violet that night in the privacy of their own room, "I found it hard to take and eat them without sharing with her, the dear, affectionate child!" he said with feeling. "But I knew it gave her pleasure to do her father that little service. Ah, it is so much pleasanter to love and indulge one's children than to reprove or punish them! Yet, I am sure it is the truest kindness to train them to obedience, as the Bible directs."

"Yes," returned Violet, "and I have often noticed that those parents who do follow that Bible teaching are more loved and respected by their children than the foolishly indulgent ones. As evidence, how devotedly fond of her father Lulu is! It delights me to see it."

"Me also, my dear," he returned with a pleased little laugh. "I doubt if any man ever had better, dearer children than mine. Nor can I believe that ever a father esteemed his greater treasures than I do mine."

The rest of the winter passed in a quiet and peaceful way to the family at Viamede. The young folks made good progress with their studies, the older ones found employment in various ways—the ladies in reading, writing letters, overseeing house and servants, and making and receiving visits; Mr. Dinsmore in much the same manner, except that he gave himself no concern about domestic affairs; while the captain found full employment in instructing his pupils and superintending work on the plantation, but allowed himself time enough to spare for participation in the fond diversions and recreations of the others.

Grandma Elsie had entirely recovered her health, and as spring opened, they began to talk of returning to their more northern homes. And, yet, they continued to tarry, looking for a visit to Viamede from the dear ones of both Ion and Fairview.

The End

Invite little Elsie Dinsmore™ Doll Over to Play!

Breezy Point Treasures' Elsie Dinsmore™ Doll brings Martha Finley's character to life in this collectible eighteen-inch all-vinyl play doll produced in conjunction with Lloyd Middleton Dolls.

The Elsie Dinsmore™ Doll comes complete with authentic Antebellum clothing and a miniature Bible. This series of books empasizes traditional family values so your and your child's character will be enriched as have millions since the 1800's.

Doll available from:

Breezy Point Treasures, Inc.
124 Kingsland Road
Hayneville, GA 31036 USA

Call for details on ordering:

1-888-487-3777

or visit our website at
www.elsiedinsmore.com